The Curse of
Camp Gray Owl

For Mimi and Mr. Clafton,
Perhaps you'll recognize
a bit of my father in the
character of "Longbow."

Patricia Edwards Clyne
March 1981

◁————The Curse of

Camp Gray Owl

Patricia Edwards Clyne

DODD, MEAD & COMPANY   NEW YORK

1 2 3 4 5 6 7 8 9 10

Library of Congress Cataloging in Publication Data

Clyne, Patricia Edwards.
  The curse of Camp Gray Owl.

  SUMMARY: Five friends explore an old Army camp
that has been cursed by an Indian.
  [1. Mystery and detective stories] I. Title.
PZ7.C6277Cu   [Fic]   80–2783
ISBN 0–396–07922–9

Dedicated to
all the boys and girls and teachers
who sent me letters expressing their
interest in the further adventures
of the five young people I wrote about
in my earlier book, Tunnels of Terror.

Author's Note

Although this is a work of fiction, there actually is an abandoned artillery range in a state park not too many miles from my home where my family and I have spent many an enjoyable afternoon exploring the tunnels and walking along the walls. And while literary license has been taken in some aspects of the actual layout, my fictional Camp Gray Owl is very much like the real one, including the story about the artillery shells that did not land where they were supposed to.

Contents

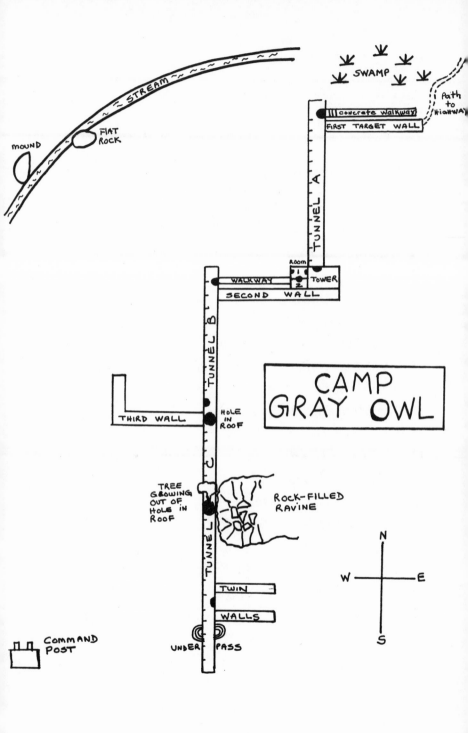

1

◁————————————— *There's No Such Thing as Ghosts*

The sultry September afternoon was without sound. Not a bird sang. Not a leaf rustled. It was as if everything in the forest had died. Even the boy and girl sat motionless on the concrete wall, staring along its length to where the wall disappeared among the trees.

Finally the boy moved.

Wiping away the drops of perspiration that clung to his upper lip, he turned to the girl beside him. "This better be worth it, Sue," he warned, "or I'll be minus one sister by nightfall."

"Oh, Andy, shut up," the girl replied calmly, as if that were the standard answer for all older brothers. Then she went on with more enthusiasm, "It'll be worth it. You'll see. And it'll be just the thing for Roy too. I know it!"

"My sister the psychiatrist!"

"And what's wrong with that?" Sue demanded.

11

"Nothing, except I've never seen a twelve-year-old psychiatrist before."

Ignoring the taunt, Sue went on earnestly, "Well, somebody's got to help Roy get out of the dumps. His parents haven't been able to do it and neither has his doctor, so I guess it's up to his friends."

Andy nodded seriously, but a grin was pulling at the corners of his mouth. "Especially if one of those friends just happens to have a crush on Roy!"

That did it. Brown ponytail flying, Sue Gregorio pounced on her brother. "You stink, Andy!" she yelped. "You stink just like that rotten old swamp down there. So why don't you go down there where you belong?"

Despite his larger size, Sue almost had succeeded in pushing Andy off the low concrete wall when another female voice cut through the steamy air.

"Are you two at it again?" Alana O'Malley called.

Sue halted in mid-shove and looked up. Through the trees she could see two teenagers picking their way along a narrow path bordering the marshy ground. The distraction gave Andy enough time to pull himself back to a more secure position, and he offered a hand to the blonde girl who was now ready to climb onto the wall.

"Sue, did your parents ever consider sending you and Andy to a home for delinquent siblings?" The question came from the other newcomer, a sandy-haired boy whose blue eyes were crinkled at the corners from the laughter he was trying to hold inside.

"What's a sibling, Chad?" Sue asked the boy, her anger apparently forgotten.

"Sibling is what you are to Andy and what Andy is to you," Chad Evans explained.

"You mean enemies?"

The three teenagers erupted with laughter, leaving Sue to regard them with a confused look on her face.

"In your case, I guess it does mean enemies," Alana said when she finally stopped laughing. "But a sibling is really a brother or sister."

Still somewhat miffed at being laughed at, Sue mumbled, "Oh, I see. Thanks for telling me, Alana." Then she asked, "Alana, didn't you and Chad bring Roy with you?"

Alana shook her head. "Roy said he'd be along a little later. He's still over at the football field watching the tryouts for the team."

"And he's eating his heart out," Chad added.

"Why doesn't Roy stay away from there?" Andy exploded. "He knows he can't play football anymore. The doctor almost wasn't able to patch up his knee the last time he hurt it—you remember back in November, when Roy was tackled during the game against South Valley High."

"Who could forget it?" Alana sighed. "That's when

13

the doctor warned Roy that if he ever plays football again he could injure his knee so badly he'd never walk right!"

"But I don't think Roy really believed the doctor then," Chad spoke up. "I think Roy felt that if he exercised his knee and got rid of the limp . . ."

"Which he did!" Andy broke in. "Even though Roy's knee still bothers him when he tries to do too much, he doesn't limp at all anymore."

"But his knee will never be strong enough for him to play football—which is exactly what the doctor told him again this past June when Roy went for his checkup."

Andy's eyes widened in understanding. "So that's what brought about the sudden change in Roy, and why he's not interested in anything, including school."

"Did Roy really say he is going to quit school?" Alana wanted to know.

Chad nodded. "He even told some of his teachers before the term ended that he was dropping out. His parents haven't been able to talk him out of it either. He's determined to quit."

"He'll do it too!" Sue declared. "Roy never says something he doesn't mean." Then turning to Andy, she added, "Not like some other people I know."

"Now don't you two start up again," Chad said as he took a seat astride the concrete wall. "Anyway,

14

it's time you told us about your idea, Sue."

"And also why you wanted us to come all the way out here in the middle of nowhere on such a hot day," Alana added as she fanned her heat-flushed face.

"What is this place anyway?" Andy chimed in.

Sue dug into the pocket of her jeans. "Here. Here's what it's all about."

Chad took the sweat-dampened paper Sue handed him and carefully unfolded it. As he did so, Andy and Alana crowded close to look at the smudged pencil lines stretching at right angles across the paper.

"Looks like some kind of geometry problem," Chad concluded. "Only instead of 'Angle A' or 'Line B,' this has things like 'Tunnel A' and 'Wall B' marked down."

"Is this one of your kooky jokes, Sue?" Andy asked in a menacing tone. "If it is . . ."

"Sue wouldn't bring us all the way out here just for a joke," Alana defended the younger girl.

"Oh, no?" Andy grunted.

"No, she wouldn't," Alana maintained. "Especially not Roy with his bad knee."

"Well, maybe not," Andy conceded. Then pointing to the paper with one hand, he poked Sue with the other. "Just what is this thing, my dear, sweet, mysterious sister?"

"It's a map!" Sue announced triumphantly. "A map of Camp Gray Owl!"

15

"You mean this place was once a Boy Scout camp?" Chad asked.

"No, an Army camp," Sue corrected. "Actually an old artillery range—and a haunted one at that!"

All of a sudden it was as silent as it had been when Andy and Sue first arrived. The three teenagers stared at the younger girl. Then they slowly turned to gaze around them at the forested hills that sloped away on either side of the concrete wall on which they sat.

Alana was the first to speak. "It *is* kind of a spooky place," she said in a low voice.

Eyes wide, Andy began to nod his head in agreement, but caught himself just in time. "You only think so because Sue said it was haunted," he declared. "There's no such things as ghosts or spooks or . . .".

Andy's voice trailed away as he became aware of another sound coming from the woods just beyond the rim of the marsh. It was a snapping sound, starting and then stopping, as if someone—or something—was making his way through the underbrush and once in a while stepped on a dry twig.

Startled glances were exchanged, then smiles as a single word burst from their throats: "Roy!"

"We're over here, Roy!" their cheery cry rang out. But there was no answering call—only the occasional snapping sound.

"Roy?" Sue's voice quavered.

16

Still nothing.

"Roy, is that you?"

After waiting several silent seconds, Alana murmured, "If it isn't Roy out there, then who . . ."

"But it is!" Sue whooped. "I see Roy now. There—over there!"

A frown creased Chad's forehead as he watched the black-haired Roy approach along the vague path they had taken earlier—a path that skirted the marshy section and was some distance away from where the snapping sounds had been heard.

"Did you get lost or something?" Andy asked the newcomer. "We heard you thrashing through the woods up there on the other side of the swamp."

"Thrashing through the woods with my bum knee?" Roy answered. "Not me. I came straight down the path from the highway just like Sue told me to do. Now will someone tell me what all this is about?"

But no one answered Roy's question. They were all staring at the woods beyond the swamp. And as they sat there listening, the snapping sound came again. . . .

2

◁——————— *One Man's Curse*
. . . Another Man's Blessing

Despite the depression which had possessed him since June, Roy Benedict had lost none of the analytical ability and quick thinking that had made him the star of last year's junior varsity football team. The apprehensive expression on the faces of his friends, their eyes focused on the same place in the woods, the occasional snapping sound he now heard—all of these things told Roy what his friends did not. And though he had no idea why the sound might be so disturbing to them, Roy's reaction was immediate and to the point.

Flicking back the thick black hair that always fell into his eyes, Roy called, "Hello! Hello out there!"

"Roy . . ." Sue began, but the older boy's voice drowned out whatever it was she wanted to say.

"Hello out there!" Roy called again. "Are you lost? Can we help you?"

When there was no answer to his questions, Roy

18

shrugged and was about to shout again. But this time Sue managed to stop him by planting a trembling hand over his mouth.

"Keep quiet, Roy!" she pleaded, and the fear in her voice was unmistakable.

Roy looked down at the much shorter girl. "What's making you so scared, Peanut?" he asked.

Hearing the nickname Roy had given her long ago caused Sue's gray eyes to flash fire. Momentarily forgetting her apprehension, she retorted angrily, "In case you haven't noticed, I'm not a peanut anymore!" Then the fear returned and she explained haltingly, "I'm scared, Roy, because who . . . whoever is out there won't answer. What if he has a gun . . . or something?"

"Why, it's not hunting season yet," Roy told her. "But even if it was, it would be better to make our presence known so we don't get mistaken for a deer."

"Whoever's out there knows we're not deer," Andy said in a low voice. "I think he . . . or it . . . has been watching us."

"So what?" Roy demanded. "We're not trespassing or anything like that. Sue, didn't you say yesterday that this is state-owned land?"

Sue slowly nodded. "But what if it's someone or something that doesn't care about things like that?" she asked. "What if it's the ghost of Camp Gray Owl?"

"The what?" Roy's surprise quickly turned to laughter—laughter which was so infectious that Alana and Chad could not help joining in. Even Andy began to grin. But Sue did not even smile.

It was Roy who first noticed the hurt expression in the younger girl's eyes. Gulping down his hilarity, he said seriously, "I'm sorry, Peanut. I wasn't laughing at you. It's just that the idea of a ghost—and a noisy one at that—well, it just struck me funny. Ghosts don't go bouncing through the bushes, and . . ."

"Then what is it out there?" Sue wanted to know.

"Well, since it didn't answer," Roy told her, "I figure it's some kind of animal. This is pretty much of a wilderness area, you know."

Alana gasped, "Animal? What kind of animal, Roy?"

"Not the kind to worry about," he stated firmly. "There aren't any dangerous animals around here. Isn't that true, Chad?"

All of them knew Chad Evans was a member of the State Hiking Association and had spent many summers backpacking in the mountains.

"Roy's right," Chad affirmed. "There haven't been any large predators like bears or wolves in this part of the state for a century or more. What we've been hearing is probably a deer or some smaller animal."

"Well, that makes me feel better," Alana smiled. "I think I could take a ghost much easier than I could a timber wolf. And speaking of ghosts, I'd like to hear about the one that's supposed to haunt Camp Gray Owl."

"Even better, let's hear why we're out here in the first place," Roy suggested. "All Sue told me on the phone yesterday was that she'd discovered something better than the Great Wall of China, and she wanted me to help her."

"Help *her?* That's not the way I heard it!" Andy burst out before he remembered Sue wanted to keep secret from Roy the real purpose of their expedition.

"And what was the way you heard it?" Roy asked quietly, as if he already sensed a plot that involved him.

Shifting uncomfortably, Andy stammered, "I . . . well, you see, Sue thought . . . I mean . . ." But try as he might, Andy could not think of an answer that would sustain the secret, so he turned to his sister. "Oh, why don't we just level with Roy?"

Roy's deep blue eyes focused on Sue's gray ones. Lowering her head, the younger girl barely mumbled, "Actually, it's you we want to help, Roy. We want to help you stay in school."

The beads of perspiration on Roy's upper lip shimmered as his mouth tightened into a harsh line. But Sue's eyes were still downcast, so she did not see this. Nor did she see the ominous clenching of Roy's fists. Therefore, she hurried on, "We know how much you hated to give up football, especially since you were counting on a football scholarship to pay your way through college. We also know history is your weak subject and that you've got tough old Miss Stitt for a teacher this coming year. But that doesn't mean you couldn't pass. That doesn't mean you should just give up. So we . . ."

"Mind your own business—all of you!" The words sizzled off Roy's tongue as if they were red-hot. "You call yourselves my friends? You're no friends of mine!"

Sue flinched, her crimsoned cheeks looking as if they had been burned by Roy's harsh words. He continued to glare at her for a minute. Then he turned his back on the group and started to climb down off the wall. But a strong hand twisted into the fabric of his shirt prevented Roy from going any farther. And when the pull on the back of his shirt forced Roy to turn around, it was Chad's steady gaze that met his.

"Sit down, Roy," Chad ordered. "If you weren't so mixed up inside, you wouldn't have said that. I know you don't mean it."

"Oh, yes, I do!" Roy thundered. "Now get your hands off me, Chad, or I'll . . ."

Even though Chad weighed as much as Roy, the black-haired boy was a good two inches taller than Chad, and was well known for his strength. But if this had entered Chad's mind, it was apparent it didn't matter in the least to him.

"I told you to sit down, Roy," Chad repeated. "You can fight me later if you want to, but right now you're going to listen to what Sue has to say. She's gone to a lot of trouble trying to help you, and the least you can do is listen. Then maybe you'll stop feeling so sorry for yourself and remember Sue really is your friend."

"We *all* are," Alana said softly. "That's why we're here, Roy."

Slowly Roy's fists unclenched and with a heavy sigh he sat back down on the concrete wall. "Okay, I'll listen," he gave in. "But nothing can change my mind about school or . . . or this!" And he gave his right knee a vicious clout that made his four friends shudder.

Not even the snapping sound in the woods broke the silence that followed Roy's display of despair. Chad waited for Sue to begin her explanation, but she just stared at Roy's knee. Finally Chad prodded her with his elbow.

"Well . . . uh, Roy . . . you see . . ." Sue stopped, unable to get her thoughts together.

Roy was calmer now, and he looked over at the seated girl. Sue's stubby fingers were nervously twisting and untwisting the laces of her hiking boots. "Go ahead, Peanut," Roy told her. "I said I'd listen."

Despite her dislike of still being regarded as a "peanut," Roy's use of the nickname gave Sue the encouragement she needed. The bottled-up words flooded out in one nonstop sentence:

"Since you'll never be able to get a football scholarship to college now, that means you'll have to get one on your grades, and even though you think you can't do that, especially because you've got Miss Stitt for history this year and she always assigns such tough term papers, you could get a good mark from her if you did a paper on Camp Gray Owl 'cause it's just the kind of original research Miss Stitt likes—at least that's what Andy and Alana told me she likes—and that way you'd see you don't have to quit school and you can go to college after all!"

Roy couldn't help smiling at the earnest, and by now totally breathless, girl. But then the unhappiness returned to his eyes and he said, "It won't work. I've made up my mind that quitting school is the only thing to do. What's the sense of a cripple . . ."

"You're no cripple, Roy Benedict!" Sue exploded. "You're just a little crippled in your head is all!"

Before Roy could retort, Andy scrambled to his feet. "You never know when to shut up, do you, Sue?"

For once, Sue did not offer her brother an argument. Instead, she pulled out the smudged map she had shown the others earlier and handed it to Roy. "Here, Roy. Take a look at the layout of Camp Gray Owl. Even if you're not interested in it for school, I'll bet you'd like to see that place, wouldn't you?"

"I know I would," Chad spoke up. "So why don't we start out now? You can tell us the rest of the story as we go."

Andy began to chuckle. "Yes, Sue, you can tell us all about the wee ghosties and goblins that go bump in the night."

"Go ahead and laugh, Andy!" Sue shot back. "There may not be such things as ghosts, just like you say. But something sure went wrong here at Camp Gray Owl—something even the United States Army couldn't handle."

"What was that?" Roy asked, as he scanned the hand-drawn map with interest.

"Some people say it's the curse put on the place by an old Indian," Sue told Roy. "It caused the Army to give up and move out years ago, and it killed some guy here just the year before last." Then cupping her hands around her mouth, Sue announced with a nasal twang, "Camp Gray Owl Expedition now leaving from Wall Number One!"

Alana was slow in rising to her feet, and by the time Chad leaned down to ask if something was wrong, the others were already several yards ahead.

"What if there really is a curse?" Alana whispered to Chad.

The sandy-haired boy shrugged as he gestured toward Roy. "Who knows? One man's curse could be another man's blessing."

"Maybe so," Alana conceded, as she and Chad fell behind the others walking along the top of the wall. "But this place does give me the creeps. I keep feeling Andy was right—that we're being watched. Watched from out there. . . ."

3

◁─────────── *Walking the Wall*

For the first time since they arrived at the long-abandoned Army camp, the five young people took a good look at the concrete wall. Almost two feet wide, the top of the wall was like an elevated road through the woods, growing progressively higher as the ground dipped down on either side. Along the northern side, a concrete walkway paralleled the wall at its base.

"Don't you think it would be easier to walk down there?" Andy asked Roy, who was in the lead.

Sue's map in hand, Roy turned around carefully. Looking past Sue toward Andy, who was third in line, Roy explained, "We can see more if we stay up high like this."

"I was afraid of that," Andy gulped, for he had never liked heights and at this point the concrete wall was nearly two stories tall.

"It's only about fifty feet more to where this wall

meets another one," Roy told him. "We'll figure out what to do from there."

"Yes, sir," Sue sang out, executing a military salute that almost threw her off balance—and off the wall.

"Watch out, Sue," cautioned Andy, who was immediately behind his sister. "If you fall, I'd have to hang onto that ponytail to save you—and that might yank out all your hair."

Glancing over her shoulder, Sue scowled at Andy. "You'd really be sorry if that happened, huh?"

"Nah!" Andy teased. "It's just that bald girls don't stand a chance with older men."

This time Sue's angry stamping foot came dangerously close to the crumbling edge of the wall. This prompted Alana to say, "Andy, why don't you change places with me? Chad wants to talk to you about something anyway."

"I do?" Chad asked.

"Yes, you do," Alana said, turning to face the bewildered boy behind her. With her back to the others, Alana silently mouthed the words "Sue" and "Roy" as she plucked at that section of her blouse immediately over her heart.

The message of "heartthrob" finally got across to Chad. "Come on, Andy," he urged. "Switch places with Alana."

When Andy had done so, Chad held a restraining

hand on his friend's shoulder until the others had gone a few yards ahead.

"Why don't you quit teasing your sister about Roy?" Chad put it bluntly. "Don't you know Sue's quite serious about him?"

Andy's lips opened to form a large "O." Then he gasped, "Sue? Roy? I know she's always had a kind of hero-worship crush on Roy. But you mean *really* serious?"

Chad nodded. "I don't think Roy is even aware of how she feels. Neither was I until Alana told me."

"You're joking, Chad," Andy insisted. "Sue's just a kid."

"Maybe in your eyes, but not in hers," Chad replied.

"But Roy's four years older than Sue," Andy persisted. "And Roy's got a girl—or at least he did up until June when he became so gloomy."

"That's beside the point, Andy. I just thought you should know you're really touching a sore spot when you tease Sue about Roy. It's no joke to her."

Andy's usually clowning expression changed to one of dead seriousness. "You know, Chad, even though Sue and I bicker like crazy, she's a pretty swell kid and I wouldn't hurt her for the world."

"That's what I figured," Chad replied. "That's why I told you."

"I just hope Sue doesn't hurt herself," Andy murmured worriedly, as he started out after the others.

By the time Andy and Chad caught up with them, Roy had reached the place where the wall ended abruptly at another, much wider wall, which led off to the south. Both walls were the same height, so it was easy for Roy to step across the narrow crack that separated the two structures.

"This has to be the first tunnel," Roy told them, as he pointed to a word scrawled next to a set of lines on Sue's map.

"Tunnel?" Alana echoed. "Where is there any tunnel?"

"Right there." Roy pointed down to the wider wall on which he was now standing. "The wall must be hollow," he explained as he fanned his face with the map he had been studying. "I think I've got this place pretty much figured out now—and it's really something. Let's sit down here and take a rest. Then we'll go see the tower." And his finger indicated another word inside a square box at the other end of the two lines marked "Tunnel A."

"I still haven't figured out the tunnel," Andy groaned, "and now Roy's talking about a tower!"

Climbing across the outstretched legs of his friends, who were all seated by now, Chad stretched out on the wider wall. "Now, let's start at the beginning," he suggested.

"It's fairly simple," Roy told them, as he handed Chad the map Sue had drawn. "The whole artillery range is a series of solid target walls connected to above-ground tunnels. The tunnels must have been used to protect the soldiers who took care of the targets."

Sue uttered an exasperated sigh. "That may be simple to you, Roy, but I still can't figure all that out, even though I'm the one who copied the map."

"See the wall we just walked on?" Roy asked. "On the north side there's a concrete walkway at the base of the wall. That was where the targets were set up. The soldiers would stay on that side of the wall, while the artillerymen would be on the other side, over there in the valley." And Roy pointed toward the south.

Sue was still puzzled. "But if the targets were set up on the north side, how could the artillerymen on the other side of the wall see what they were aiming at? The wall would be in the way."

Roy laughed. "The targets would be set up on top of the wall, where we were just walking. And if the soldiers down below wanted to go from one target wall to another, they used the connecting tunnels."

When Roy finished, Sue still looked bewildered. "I think I need a compass!" she moaned. "No wonder old Gray Owl cursed the place!"

"Now, that's the part I'm most interested in," Alana

spoke up. "And I'm not going to go any farther until you tell us about the ghost."

Andy sighed, "Ghost stories on a hot September day! Where did you hear all this anyway, Sue?"

"You remember last month when the Parks Commissioner visited Dad, don't you? Well, since Dad's on the Town Planning Board, the Commissioner wanted him to know the state was again thinking about selling this land to a private developer for a housing complex. It seems someone else had wanted to buy the land a couple of years ago, but before the deal could go through, the man was found dead out here. Our local paper wrote a story saying maybe the man was a victim of the curse of Camp Gray Owl.

"That interested me," Sue went on, "so I asked Dad if I could look at the folder full of material the Parks Commissioner gave him to read. That newspaper story—along with a map—was inside. It seems that back in the early 1900s the Army bought up this land for an artillery range—you know, a place for the soldiers to have target practice. But before they could start building it, some old Indian who lived here said they couldn't do it because the land was sacred to his people—something about burial mounds and such."

"Burial mounds!" Alana exclaimed. "I wonder if my father knows about that!"

"I never heard him mention it," Chad spoke up. "And last summer I took one of his classes in amateur archaeology. Roy did too." Then realizing that Sue was impatient to go on, Chad motioned for her to continue her story.

"The Army wouldn't listen to the old Indian," Sue resumed, "and they gave him a month to pack up his things and leave. When he didn't, they went to evict him, and found him dying. The official report was that he died of pneumonia, but some people said he just willed himself to die. Anyway, before he died, he put a curse on the artillery range and on anyone who disturbed the graves of his ancestors."

"Brrrr!" Alana said with a shiver.

Sue nodded in agreement, then continued, "I guess the Army felt kind of guilty about the way the old Indian died because they named the place for him— Camp Gray Owl. But that didn't do any good, because when the artillery range was built, nothing seemed to go right."

"How so?" Roy asked.

"Artillery shells that were aimed at the target area sometimes hit houses miles away on the outskirts of our town. This happened even though the guns weren't supposed to be able to shoot that far. There were other problems too, but mostly it was those artillery shells landing in places they weren't meant to. The Army couldn't explain how that happened either. And no matter how many changes they made in the range, the shells still kept damaging private property."

"Was anyone in town ever injured by one of those misplaced shells?" Alana wanted to know.

"Apparently not, but the people were afraid someone eventually would be killed. So they forced the Army to leave, and the land was given to the state."

"And that was the end of the curse of Camp Gray Owl?" Alana asked.

"Not quite." Sue shook her head. "So long as the place was left alone, nothing happened. But then two years ago some real-estate developer wanted to buy it."

"Don't tell me that was the guy they found in the marsh?" Chad broke in.

"Yes," Sue affirmed. "The official cause of death was drowning. But since there was only a couple of inches of water in the swamp when he died, a lot of people thought it was the curse still working."

Despite the sticky afternoon heat, goose bumps quickly spread over Alana's bare arms. Noticing this, Chad abandoned the clump of moss he had been using as a pillow and started to say, "I'll only believe that if . . ."

"If the owl hoots," Sue murmured. However, nobody

heard her because a wild shout from Andy suddenly filled the air.

"That's it! That's the opening to the tunnel!" he cried. "Look down there!"

4

◁——*The Coffin-shaped Tower*

Where the narrow target wall met the wider wall, a "T" shape was formed. The wider wall provided the arms of this "T," with one arm extending south for as far as the overlapping tree branches would allow the five young people to see. The other arm of the "T"—the one which pointed to the north—was just a dozen feet in length.

While the others were talking, Andy had peered down into the north angle of the "T." His shout brought the others to his side and they took turns leaning over the edge of the high wall in order to see what had caused his excitement.

Far below them, there was an opening in that part of the wall forming the short arm of the "T." The concrete walkway which paralleled the base of the target wall ended in six steps that descended to the opening in the wider wall.

36

"That's the tunnel all right," Roy confirmed. "But let's go see the tower first. Then we can come back here and explore the tunnel."

"Good idea," Chad agreed. And taking Alana by the hand, he began walking south along the flat top of the wall that housed the tunnel.

They had gone no more than fifty yards when they were forced to clamber through the leafy arms of a scraggly tree which had somehow taken root in a crack at the edge of the concrete structure. Once past that, they had a clear view along the remaining length of the wall.

"Wow! Will you look at that!"

Contrasting sharply with the gray concrete and the green foliage, a tall tower of deep red brick rose high above the place where the wall terminated. The upper part of the tower narrowed to a flat point, so that it resembled a coffin standing on end. Set in the side of the tower facing them was an opening like a window, but there were no panes of glass to reflect the errant sunbeams that seemed to be swallowed up as soon as they entered the gaping hole.

Taking turns poking their heads inside the window, the young people could see thick beams of rusted steel that zigzagged from wall to wall across the interior space of the otherwise empty tower.

"These steel beams look like the framework for a

staircase," Chad said. When Roy nodded his agreement, Chad went on, "I suppose this was some kind of an observation tower. Wish I could get to the top. Bet there'd be quite a view from up there."

"And quite a fall to down there," Sue pointed out, her gaze directed at the floor of the tower far below them.

"With no steps in the staircase, you'd have to shinny up the framework," Roy observed. "But for an experienced mountain goat like you, that shouldn't be any problem."

Chad grinned at Roy's half-joking compliment. "Well, maybe I'll try it if the frame is sturdy enough. I'll check it when we get inside the tower."

"And how are we going to do that?" Sue asked worriedly. "By climbing through this window and sliding down that framework?"

"I guess we could do that," Chad teased, "but I imagine it'd be easier to go through the tunnel. It figures that there's an opening between the tunnel and the tower."

"My thought exactly," Roy said. "So let's backtrack to the target wall where it isn't so high. We can climb down there and go along that concrete walkway to where those steps lead down to the tunnel opening."

The hazy September afternoon had become even more humid than before, and the forest retained its unnatural silence as the five set out to retrace their steps. Not once did they hear the snapping sound in the woods. Only the scuffing of their boots on the concrete could be heard, along with the muted tinkle of the lightweight chains that secured the lids to their canteens.

The heat, plus the quick pace Roy was setting, robbed them of any desire for conversation. So it was not until they had reached the place where the target wall was lowest that any word was spoken. Even then it was only a brief but plaintive cry from Sue:

"Hey! Wait for me!"

The others had easily jumped down from the top of the wall to the concrete walkway. But the much shorter Sue remained standing above them, unsure of how to go about it.

Andy looked up impatiently. "You sure can act like a girl sometimes!" he snorted, much to the amusement of the others—even Sue. But he was first to reach up to catch his sister, after telling her to sit down on the edge of the wall, then scoot off.

After she had safely landed, they started along the walkway, the target wall on their left looming higher and higher above them as the ground sloped down.

"The Army sure didn't leave anything behind," Roy observed. "Wouldn't you think there might be something—maybe just an old rusted helmet—that . . ."

"That you could use to illustrate your term paper for Miss Stitt!" Sue finished the sentence for him. "Don't worry, Roy," she rushed on. "We'll find something you can use. There's bound to be loads of art-tracks all around!"

Sue's mixup of words—something she often did when she was excited—was what prevented any angry outburst from Roy. And although his frown showed that he resented her refusal to accept the fact he was going to quit school, Roy only sighed and said, "I think you mean artifacts, Peanut. Not art-tracks."

It was Sue's turn to frown. But instead of making some snappy remark about the nickname "Peanut," she said cheerfully, "Art-tracks or artifacts—let's go find some!"

By this time they had reached the steps leading down to the tunnel entrance. They could feel a cool, moist draft coming from the opening, and there was a dank, earthy smell in the air.

"Well, at least it will be cool in there," Chad said as he wiped his perspiring face.

"Cool and *dark!*" Alana stressed. "Did anyone think to bring a flashlight along?"

"Nobody told us to!" Andy declared. Then as he glared at his sister, he added, "We didn't even know where we were going!"

"You never do, Andy!" Sue shot back, but her expression was apologetic when she looked at her other three companions.

Roy, who had been standing closest to the tunnel entrance, held up two fingers. "Peace!" he intoned. "If you two can stop bickering long enough, you'll find out we don't really need flashlights to walk through the tunnel."

The three other teenagers converged on the narrow tunnel entrance, crowding out Sue, who could not see over their shoulders. Plopping herself down on the top step, the younger girl impatiently waited to learn what it was Roy was talking about. From their abbreviated exclamations about "ventilation slits in the wall," "light coming in," and "all the way down the tunnel," she had just about figured it out. But then another, inhuman sound reached Sue's ears, and she momentarily forgot the conversation of her friends.

"Whooooo . . ."

Sue's gray eyes became as round as those of the owl that might have made the sound. Unaware that Chad had turned around to make room for her at the tunnel entrance, Sue stared toward the forested hillside.

"Come on, Sue," Chad called. "We're waiting for you."

But the young girl made no move as the soft, throaty sound was repeated.

"Whooooo . . . whooooo . . ."

Chad heard it too and laughed, "That's just an old hoot owl out there in the woods."

Sue nodded and came down the steps to the tunnel entrance. "Just an owl." She echoed Chad's words as she followed him into the tunnel. But as she cast one last look over her shoulder, she murmured, "I sure hope that's all it is. . . ."

5

The tunnel was tall enough for them to stand upright, and the floor was of hard-packed earth that should have made walking no problem. But the shafts of light coming in through the long narrow slits along one side of the tunnel wall patterned the darkness in a way that was more confusing than helpful. Yet these slits, cut high into the right-hand wall at intervals of every nine feet, provided their only light, so the explorers were thankful for it.

Much of the time, however, the floor of the tunnel was obscured in darkness. At such times Roy, still in the lead, would carefully slide one booted foot in front of the other, never putting his weight on it until he was sure he was on unobstructed solid ground. In this slow and painstaking manner, they traveled along the concrete corridor, frequently shuffling through clumps

43

of dead leaves that had blown in through the ventilation slits in the west wall.

Concentrating on the ground, none of them said a word until there was a soft thump, followed by a low groan.

In the dim light between two slits in the tunnel wall, Roy stood rubbing his forehead. "I bumped into that," he said, pointing to a shallow metal box attached to the opposite wall. "I didn't see it, and when I . . ."

"That's the trouble," Chad broke in. "We can't see well enough in here without flashlights. We might never have known that box was there unless you bumped into it, Roy. And we may be missing a lot of other stuff as well. That's why I think we should call it a day and come back tomorrow with proper equipment."

"But what if Roy won't . . ."

Even though Sue did not finish her sentence, Chad understood what she meant. "I think Roy's just as interested in seeing what else is in here, aren't you, Roy?" he said.

Roy's answer came in the form of a question: "What do you think that metal box was used for?" Then he added, "Maybe tomorrow we can find out."

Chad looked over at Sue, who was smiling broadly at Roy's obvious intention of returning to Camp Gray Owl. "Okay," she said. "If someone will lead the way out, we'll head for home."

Having become accustomed to the cool dampness of the tunnel, they were not ready for the humid air that enveloped them when they emerged. Therefore, they all agreed to call a short halt and have a drink from their canteens before continuing their journey home.

As they sat on the steps that led from the tunnel entrance to the concrete walkway, Alana mentioned the metal box, and Roy and Chad began discussing what it might have been used for. They had gotten no further than deciding to mark its location on their map, when Roy discovered something that made all of them forget about the metal box.

"The map!" Roy exclaimed. "Where's Sue's map? Have you got it, Chad?"

"I gave it back to you when we started into the tunnel," Chad reminded him.

Roy nodded. "Yes, now I remember. In fact, I remember taking it out of my pocket just before . . . Oh, no! I must have dropped it when I hit my head!"

"Well, here we go again," Sue said, standing up. "Back into the tunnel."

"Not me," Andy stated flatly. "I'm too hot, and we've still got a long walk home. Your old map will be safe in there until we come back tomorrow."

"It will be easier to find then too," Alana pointed out. "We'll have flashlights with us tomorrow."

Sue was unconvinced. "But what if someone else finds it?"

Andy laughed. "Who? This place is deserted, remember?"

The doubt in Sue's eyes remained. "But what if it rains during the night?" she persisted.

"So what if it does rain?" Alana asked.

"The tunnel could get flooded, that's what!" Sue snapped. "Don't you remember what happened in Pompey's Cave?"

Sue's reference to the time they had been trapped in a flooding cave swept the smiles from the faces of her four companions. Their expressions were serious as she went on earnestly, "If the tunnel flooded, my map would be lost forever!"

Andy reached up to tug at his sister's ponytail. "Calm down, Sue. The weatherman didn't say anything about rain. But even if it did rain, there's little chance of the tunnel getting flooded. It's not deep underground like Pompey's Cave was. Anyway, you could always draw another map."

Slapping away Andy's hand, Sue almost shouted, "I can't! I can't draw another map!"

"Why?" came Roy's question.

"Because the Parks Commissioner met with my father again last week and he took back the folder full

46

of material he had left for Dad to look at. The map was in that folder!"

With that, Sue leaped down the steps to the tunnel entrance. "Well, is anybody coming with me to get the map?"

"Too hot," Alana told her.

"Got to give this knee a rest," was Roy's excuse.

"It isn't gonna rain anyway," Andy insisted.

Sue glanced up at Chad, but any hope she might have had that he would accompany her into the tunnel was quickly dashed. Stretched out on the concrete walkway, with his canvas-covered canteen serving as a pillow, Chad lazily waved one hand. "We'll wait for you," he yawned.

"Some friends!" Sue muttered as she entered the dim interior of the tunnel.

Gathering clouds had obscured the hazy sunshine so that much less light was coming in through the slits in the west wall of the tunnel. Not only was the tunnel much darker now, but without her other companions, it seemed much larger to Sue. Still she went on.

Sue had reached the twentieth slit—she knew, for she had been counting them—when she heard the shuffling sound. At first she tried to ignore it, telling herself it was just an echo of her own feet in the leaves that dotted the earthen floor. But echoes occur right away, and she continued to hear the shuffling sound long moments after she stopped next to the metal box where Roy had bumped his head.

"Roy . . . Andy?" she barely whispered. "Chad?"

Then raising her voice, Sue demanded, "Who's there? Andy, if you're trying to scare me, I'll . . ."

There was no answer, but there was no shuffling sound either. So with a determined frown on her freckled forehead, Sue knelt down to search for the lost map. Unable to see a thing on the floor, she gingerly ran her hand down the rough concrete wall below the metal box. Then gritting her teeth to hold back visions of spiders and snakes that crawled into her thoughts, she forced her fingers to explore the damp ground.

Finally her hand brushed against something more substantial than the crumbling leaves that littered the floor. Was it the map? It certainly felt like the folded piece of paper Roy had lost, and Sue's fingers closed around it. As they did, she heard the shuffling sound again.

Sue stared back down the length of the tunnel to where a small gray rectangle of light marked the far-off entrance. All she could hear was her own rapid breathing.

"I must have made that shuffling sound myself," she murmured, "when I found the map in the leaves."

48

But was it really the map or just some old piece of paper? In order to find out, Sue went over to the nearest slit in the west wall where enough light filtered in for her to see.

It was the map all right, and she grinned happily— but only for a moment. For then she heard the shuffling once more, and this time she knew she hadn't caused the sound.

The soft swish came from somewhere down the tunnel—somewhere between the entrance and where she was standing!

"Andy . . . Roy . . . is it you?" she called weakly.

When there was no response, Sue's voice took on a pleading tone, "Come on, guys, answer me. You've made your point. You scared me. Now let's go home!"

The damp air hung around her, heavy and silent, until the shuffling sound started up again. It was coming toward her from the inky shadows of the tunnel, blocking her way back to the entrance. It was cutting her off from the safety of the outside world!

Sue screamed for her friends. But even as she did so she knew they couldn't hear her. The concrete walls of the tunnel were at least a foot thick, and the ventilation slits were on the opposite side from where the other four were waiting for her outside the entrance. And she was too far within the tunnel for her screams to reach them from inside.

There was only one thing for her to do—run! Run farther along the tunnel—into the part they had not explored. Hadn't Chad or Roy said something about the tunnel being connected to the tower? If she could get into the tower, maybe she could climb the steel framework to where the window overlooked the top of the wide wall.

And so the terrified Sue raced blindly down the darkened corridor, sometimes stumbling over the uneven ground, all the time praying there would be no obstacle to trip her.

By now the pulse was pounding so hard in her ears Sue could no longer hear the shuffling sound. But it was there—she was sure of that. And it was coming after her.

If only she could get to the tower before it caught up with her . . .

6

◁——— *What Happened to Sue?*

Unlike Chad, whose favorite resting position was flat on his back, Roy was neither relaxed nor comfortable as he sat on the top step outside the tunnel entrance. Staring at his friend stretched out on the concrete walkway, Roy snorted, "Chad, I think you could even sleep on a bed of nails!"

"Yup," Chad murmured agreeably, but his eyes remained closed.

Nearby, Alana and Andy were sitting with their backs against the target wall, arms encircling their upraised knees. Andy only chuckled at Chad's reply, but Alana had caught the irritation in Roy's voice. Raising her head from where it had been resting on her knees, she asked, "What's wrong, Roy?"

"Nothing," Roy muttered. He was on his feet now, pacing the narrow width of the concrete walkway.

51

"Your knee bothering you, Roy?" Alana inquired softly.

His blue eyes intent on the tunnel entrance, Roy burst out, "No, not my knee. It's Sue that's bothering me. She should have been back by now."

Andy's head shot up at the same time Chad's eyes blinked open. "You know, you're right, Roy," Chad spoke first. "She's been in there a mighty long time."

"She probably can't find the map in the dark, and she's still in there searching," Alana reasoned. "You know how determined Sue can be when she feels something's important."

Alana had been looking directly at Roy when she said this, and her meaning was not lost on him. "That Sue's quite a gal," he agreed. "But it's time we started for home, so I'll give her a shout."

He was down the steps in a flash. Standing inside the tunnel entrance, he called Sue's name, then waited for her answer. When none came, he shouted again, this time much louder. There was still no response, so he uttered a shrill whistle which echoed through the concrete corridor. But that was the only echo they heard, and when the echo died, there was silence.

Roy stepped outside, shrugging his shoulders at the three teenagers looking down at him from the concrete walkway.

"I think we should check on her," Alana said, rising to her feet.

Roy held up a hand. "No sense in all of us going in there," he told them. Then lowering his eyes, he explained, "I should have been the one to go back for the map in the first place. After all, I'm the one who lost it! So I'll go look for Sue."

Chad nodded understandingly, but his voice was firm when he said, "We'd better all go."

Andy opened his mouth to say something. However, when he saw the serious look on Chad's face, he fell silently into line behind Alana.

The cooler air inside the tunnel made their sweat-dampened clothes feel clammy, and even the well-built Chad shivered. As they waited for their eyes to adjust to the gloomy interior, Alana and Roy took turns calling out Sue's name. But again there was no answer.

"I just can't understand it," Roy said worriedly. "Surely Sue can hear us. She was only going as far as that metal box on the wall."

"Maybe that's it," Chad said grimly. "Maybe she went farther into the tunnel."

Andy gulped. "She wouldn't. Not alone."

"But what if . . ." Alana's voice trailed off into the shadows surrounding them, and she pressed against Roy who was in front of her. "Hurry up, Roy," she urged. "We don't have to go so slowly. Even if it's dark in here, we know we've got a clear pathway— at least up to the metal box."

But Roy needed no urging. Despite the darkness, he hurried down the concrete corridor. The three other young people stumbled along behind him, their concern for Sue overriding their usual caution.

His left arm extended so that his hand brushed the concrete wall as he went along, Roy touched the metal box before he actually saw it.

"Here it is," he panted. "But no Sue."

The others did not answer. They just followed Roy as he continued down the tunnel, shouting out Sue's name every few minutes. They were forced to go more slowly now, not only because this section of the tunnel was unfamiliar, but because it sloped downward slightly and was more littered with leaves.

When it seemed to all of them as if the tunnel would never end, they were brought to an abrupt halt by Roy's rasping announcement:

"I see light!"

"Where?" Chad asked.

"In the center of the tunnel up ahead. It's not much, but it's coming from something larger than one of those ventilation slits."

Chad brushed past Alana to stand beside Roy. Eyes focused on the dim rectangle of light ahead of them,

54

he said, "Maybe it's an opening to the tower."

"Maybe," Roy nodded. "Let's go see."

For some reason—possibly fear of what they might find—the four explorers slowly approached the lighted area at the end of the tunnel. This time they did not call out Sue's name, and it was this silence that enabled them to hear a low whimper—a whimper that came from beyond the end of the tunnel.

7

◁——————————————— *Rescue on
the Swaying Stair*

Roy was the first to step through the low doorway at
the end of the tunnel, emerging into what was, indeed,
the tower. This time they were at the very bottom of
the tall, coffin-shaped structure. High above them they
could see the large window they had looked through
earlier from the outside. Zigzagging across the interior
space of the tower rose the rusted steel framework of
what had once been a staircase. And clinging to that
part of the framework up near the window was a shiver-
ing, whimpering figure.

"Sue!"

The brown ponytail moved, and two fear-filled gray
eyes peered down at them over arms tightly wrapped
around the rusted steel beam.

"Sue, how in the world did you get up there?" Andy
burst out.

The whimper became a sob.

"Hush, Andy," Alana whispered. "Can't you see she's scared half to death?" Then raising her voice, Alana called softly, "It's all right, Sue. We're here. You can come down now."

Sue made no move to climb down the steel framework. She only sobbed harder.

"Come on, Sue, it's safe," Chad urged.

"Sure it is," Roy added. "Climb down, Sue."

Between sobs, Sue managed to call, "But I can't . . . I can't climb down!"

Chad turned to Roy, whispering, "She must be frozen up there. I've seen it happen to rock climbers—they manage to climb up, but then they get scared and can't climb down."

"Then I'll go up and get her," Roy stated.

His words were loud enough for Sue to hear, and she called down, "Don't . . . don't do it, Roy. It's shaky. The frame's come loose from the wall!"

Sue's concern for Roy had momentarily triumphed over her terror. But that terror returned as soon as Roy touched one of the two steel beams that slanted down to the floor of the tower.

"Don't!" Sue screamed, almost losing her grip on the beam.

"Easy, Sue," Roy called up to her. "We're going to get you down safely. Just hold on tightly until we figure something out."

Chad had gone over to the wall containing the window. Looking up, he could see where the steel frame had once been bolted to the wall just below the window. However, the bolts had pulled loose from the wall, leaving an open space of several feet between the window and the rusted steel to which Sue clung. Still attached to the upper end of this slanted framework, another pair of steel beams stretched horizontally across the width of the tower, with their ends anchored to the opposite wall.

"There's no way to get to her from the outside," Chad reported as he rejoined his friends. "There's too much space between the window up there and the stair frame. Anyway, it would take too much time to walk back through the tunnel to the outside, then return along the top of the wall to the tower window."

"Sue couldn't possibly hang on up there that long," Alana agreed.

"Maybe we could get her to jump and we could catch her," Andy suggested. "Just like we did back at the target wall."

Roy shook his head. "That was a shorter jump back there. It's at least thirty feet up to where Sue is now. Much too high for a safe catch."

Walking over to where the base of the steel stair frame touched the ground, Roy announced, "I'm going up after her."

"No, you're not," Andy argued. "She's my sister. It's my responsibility."

"You have no experience in climbing, Andy," Chad told him. "And you don't like heights anyway. I've done some mountain climbing, so I'm the logical one to . . ."

Roy's grip on his shoulder caused Chad to stop talking. "You may be a mountain climber, Chad, but it's strength that's needed here, and I'm stronger than you."

"But your knee . . ." Alana started to say.

Roy either did not hear Alana or he chose to ignore her reminder, for when he spoke, his words were directed at Chad. "It's my fault Sue's up there," he said. "It's my job to rescue her."

Without a word, Chad stepped back. Motioning to Andy to hold on to the other leg of the stair frame, Chad straddled the steel beam Roy would climb, putting all his weight on the end nearest the ground. "We'll hold it as steady as we can, Roy," he said finally. "Good luck."

Taking a deep breath, Roy called up to Sue, "I'm coming to get you now. Just hang on until I get there. The frame may sway a little, but don't get frightened. It'll be okay."

"Don't . . . don't do it, Roy!" Sue screamed. "You'll get hurt all over again!"

"No, I won't," Roy called back. "Don't you trust me, Peanut?"

"I . . . I . . . Sure, I do . . . but . . ."

"Then there's nothing to worry about, is there?" Roy answered as confidently as he could.

But there was plenty to worry about as Roy began to shinny up the slanted steel beam. So long as he was near the bottom, his added weight caused the end of the steel beam to bite further into the dirt floor of the tower. However, as he progressed up the rusted frame, the unattached upper end near the window began to shift, and a grating sound filled the air.

Roy knew the most perilous time would occur when he reached Sue—when their combined weight would place added stress on the already weakened framework. If Sue suddenly shifted on the steel beam, or fought his attempt to guide her back down . . . Pushing these thoughts to the back of his mind, Roy concentrated on reassuring Sue as he pulled himself up to where she clung.

At first Sue would not ease her hold on the beam, and Roy had uneasy visions of what might happen if he tried to pry her rigid arms loose. But finally Sue became more confident as Roy's strong arms encircled her body from behind, and she reached back to hook her left arm around his neck.

"Okay, Peanut," he told her. "Keep your other arm around the beam, but not too tightly. We're going to kind of slide back down."

Sue gasped when the beam swayed sickeningly, and her whole body jerked as the framework gave a metallic groan.

"No quick moves, Peanut," came Roy's whisper close to her ear. "You're doing fine. The swaying will stop soon. Just keep sliding down along with me."

Below them, the other three young people held their breath. For they saw what Roy could not. The other end of the horizontal beams—the beams that had been bolted to the opposite wall—seemed to be coming loose from their mooring.

A dull thud sounded on the dirt floor next to Alana, and she looked down to see a large rusty bolt that had fallen from the groaning, swaying stair. Terror clutched at her heart and she wanted to run. But she was unable to tear her eyes from the heavy iron bolt that had landed just a few feet away from where she stood. Because of this, she did not see Chad raise his arms to help Sue off the steel beam. Only when the metallic groaning slowed down, then ceased altogether, did Alana look up.

"You're safe!" she cried.

The panting Roy was unable to answer, and Sue's

head was buried in her brother's embrace. So it was left up to Chad to voice the thought that was in all their minds:

"Let's get out of here!"

As they made their way back through the tunnel, Sue told them about the shuffling sound she had heard, and how she had tried to escape it by racing down the tunnel and into the tower. It was not until she had climbed up the steel beam that she realized it offered no exit to the window in the tower wall. By that time she was too frightened to climb back down.

"And anyway," Sue added, "there was still that thing back in the tunnel—whatever it was."

"Are you sure there was something following you, Sue?" Chad asked skeptically.

"I heard it, Chad. I heard it shuffling through the leaves on the floor."

"Couldn't it have been some animal, or . . ."

"Or my imagination?" Sue interrupted. "Do you think I'm making all this up?"

By this time they had reached the outside opening to the tunnel, and Chad motioned for Sue to take a seat on one of the steps leading up to the concrete walkway.

"I'm not suggesting any such thing," he told the indignant girl. "It's just that there wasn't anything moving inside the tunnel when we went in there the

62

first time. And we never left the entrance after we came out. When you went back in, Sue, all four of us remained right here, and we could have seen anything entering the tunnel."

"And you've got to admit that nothing very large could squeeze through those ventilation slits in the tunnel wall," Roy pointed out. "So how could anything have been in there, Sue?"

Sue glanced from Roy to Chad, then back to Roy again. "I did hear something," she repeated, but this time she sounded less positive.

"I'm sure you did," Alana spoke up. "But sometimes a simple thing—like the wind stirring up leaves—can sound like something terrible."

"Especially if you're all alone in a dark tunnel," Roy told Sue.

"Well, maybe you're right that it wasn't really anything," Sue conceded. "And I guess I should be glad that it wasn't, because we still want to explore that tunnel with flashlights, don't we?"

The four teenagers stared at the younger girl in disbelief. "You mean you'd go back in there?" Andy gasped.

"Sure!" Sue declared. "That is, as long as you guys are with me. After all, we want to find some art-tracks for Roy, don't we?"

Without waiting for a reply, Sue handed Roy the map she had retrieved from the tunnel. Then climbing the remaining steps, she set out along the concrete walkway. "We'd better get home," she called over her shoulder. "We've got a big day tomorrow!"

The others followed as Sue led the way out of Camp Gray Owl. Evening shadows were stretching dark fingers over the small valley and an owl hooted somewhere behind them. But this time the night bird's call did not disturb any of the tired travelers, nor was there any snapping sound coming from the wooded hillside. There was only the murmur of Chad and Alana's voices as they fell far enough behind not to be overheard by Roy.

"That climb up the steel beam proved to Roy that his knee isn't quite the handicap he thinks it is," Chad was saying.

"Maybe so," Alana replied quietly. "But is that going to make him change his mind about quitting school?"

When Chad did not answer, Alana went on, "I'm afraid it's not just a history course that Roy's afraid of failing. That's just the tip of the iceberg."

"Iceberg?" Chad repeated.

"Yes. You know how the greatest and most dangerous part of an iceberg is beneath the water where it can't be seen. Well, Roy's problem is like that. What can be seen is his trouble with history—and Roy is using that as his reason for quitting school. But I think the biggest part of the problem is his depression over his knee. He considers himself a total failure, so he's just given up on everything."

Chad frowned. "Then you don't think Sue's idea about finding some artifacts . . ."

"Oh, I hope we do find some!" Alana declared. "It could be a start in getting Roy interested in things again—but only a start."

Chad silently regarded Roy's broad-shouldered back several yards ahead of them on the trail to the highway. "We've still got a long way to go," Chad finally murmured, but he did not mention whether he was referring to their journey home or to Roy.

8

◁————— *Great Expectations*
. . . Greater Disappointment

During the night a Canadian air mass moved in over the northeastern United States. It brought with it cooler temperatures and a clarity of sky that made the long walk to Camp Gray Owl seem much shorter for the five explorers the next morning. This time they made the journey together, armed with flashlights, food, and even a canvas shopping bag. The latter item had been Sue's idea. "Just in case we find something," she explained, as they made their way along the path skirting the swamp.

"Hush!"

The single syllable sliced through the air, causing Sue to look in amazement at Alana, who had issued the order. But the older girl had her face turned away from Sue, and she was staring across the swamp toward the wooded hillside.

66

"What's wrong?" Chad whispered. "What did you hear?"

Her eyes still on the thick green foliage, Alana answered, "That's just it. I don't hear anything."

"Huh?" came Roy's questioning grunt.

Alana faced her four companions. "Doesn't it seem kind of strange to you," she went on, "that it's so quiet—no birds singing or anything?"

"Maybe they're all out hunting worms," was Andy's cheerful suggestion.

"Or maybe they've already flown south," Sue offered. "It is September, you know."

Alana was shaking her head. "Not all birds fly south for the winter. So why don't we hear any?"

Chad frowned. "I don't know the answer to that one, except maybe . . ."

"Except maybe Camp Gray Owl is haunted!" Sue said excitedly. "Just like the story said it was!"

Nobody, not even Andy, laughed at Sue's mention of Camp Gray Owl's sinister past.

"I'm sure there's a much more scientific explanation," Chad stated a bit gruffly. "Birds don't sing all the time anyway."

Just then—as if to mock him—the voice of a single bird sounded in the woods. It was not the lilting call of a songbird, however. Instead, it was the low, throaty hoot of an owl.

Roy seemed startled for a moment. Then with a half-grin, he said, "See, there's at least one bird."

Glancing up at him quizzically, Sue asked, "But aren't owls night birds?"

"What difference does it make?" Andy spoke up.

Sue frowned at her brother. "The difference is that the old Indian is supposed to haunt this place in the form of an owl! And if real owls aren't awake in the daytime, that means . . ."

"That means we must have been standing here all day jabbering about birds and now it's nighttime!" Andy shot back.

Before Sue could issue a retort, Chad pointed at the concrete walkway that led to the tunnel. "Andy's right," he said. "We're wasting time." Glancing from Sue to Roy and then back at Sue, Chad added in a low voice, "And we've only got three more days until school starts!"

Chad's meaning was unmistakable. They had only three more days to find some way of convincing Roy not to quit school.

Thus reminded of their main reason for coming to Camp Gray Owl, Sue immediately set off down the concrete walk, acting as if she had forgotten all about the owl. The others matched her quick pace and within minutes they had entered the tunnel.

With strong sunlight flooding in through the ventilation slits, and their flashlights illuminating the darkened areas in between, the tunnel was no longer the mysterious place it had been on their earlier trip.

For a brief time their excitement was aroused when their flashlights revealed a hole in the floor where it joined the base of the west wall. Since it was in a darkened area between two ventilation slits, it would have been impossible for them to have seen the hole yesterday, even if they had been looking for it.

Roy was about to switch his light back to the center of the passageway when Sue put a restraining hand on his wrist. "Wait a minute, Roy," she urged. "Let's take a better look at that hole."

As the other three waited, Roy obligingly concentrated the strong beam of his battery lantern on the U-shaped hole in the dirt floor. Sue was on her knees, one hand resting on the rim of the hole and the other braced against the concrete wall, peering into the earthen cavity.

"It doesn't go straight down," she cried. "It curves under the wall and leads to the outside!" Jumping to her feet, she went on excitedly, "Remember yesterday when I heard someone in here? Remember you said there couldn't have been anyone in the tunnel between me and the entrance because there was no other way to get in? Well, that hole proves . . ."

"It doesn't prove anything," Roy interrupted Sue.

"The hole's too small for someone to crawl in from the outside."

Chad nodded as he said, "Roy's right, Sue. The hole was probably dug by some kind of burrowing animal, like a mole or . . ."

"Oh, come on, Chad!" Sue exploded. "Even I know that a tiny animal like a mole wouldn't need to dig a hole that wide!"

"How about blaming Mother Nature?" Alana asked quickly but calmly, again assuming the role of peace-maker for the group. "Isn't it possible that the hole was caused by rainwater seeping under the wall and eroding away the dirt?"

But Sue wasn't about to accept this either. Staring down into the U-shaped opening, she murmured, "Something came through that hole yesterday. I'm sure of it. Something that followed me and stopped when-ever I stopped, then started whenever I started . . ."

"My big brave sister!" Andy chuckled. "Scared by a mole!"

"It wasn't any mole, Andy!" Sue's angry voice ech-oed through the tunnel. "It was . . . it was a . . ."

Roy positioned his thick-set body in between the bickering brother and sister. "Maybe we can find out what it was," he told Sue. "But we can only do that if we continue looking. So let's get going, huh?"

However, there was no answer evident as they went

on with their search. Nor was there even much to look at. "In fact, today's journey through the tunnel is rather dull," Chad whispered to Alana, after the group had proceeded for more than a hundred feet and had found nothing except clumps of decaying leaves.

This feeling was reinforced when they reached the shallow, rectangular box attached to the wall halfway down the tunnel. What had seemed so large in the darkness yesterday turned out to be nothing more than a metal box about a foot wide and two feet long. No lock secured its door, which swung open with a rusty squeak when Roy touched it. Except for a lacy gray spider web stretched across one corner and a few pieces of copper wire partially sheathed in time-disintegrated rubber, the box was empty.

"Wouldn't you think the Army would have left something behind?" Roy repeated his disappointed comment of the day before.

"I'm sure the Army did leave something," Sue told him. "We just haven't found it yet."

But even Sue's optimism had faded by the time they reached the end of the tunnel and entered the tower. While there were a few pieces of rotted wood lying around, and even an old rusted gasoline can in one pile of leaves, nothing that would serve as a souvenir—or as a display to accompany a term paper—could be found.

"It's still an exciting place, though, isn't it?" Sue asked in a strained voice, as she looked worriedly at Roy.

There was sympathy in Alana's blue eyes when she nodded to the younger girl. "Sure, Sue, it's a great place. And even if there's nothing here in the tower, there's still a lot more of Camp Gray Owl for us to explore."

"And how!" came Roy's exclamation. "I just found another doorway!"

9

◁──────── *A Gift from the Past*

When they had been in the tower the day before, the five explorers had been too upset to notice the low doorway in the wall adjacent to the tunnel opening. Now that they had seen it, they rushed over and were about to step through it when Chad's voice halted them.

"Better shine our lights in there first," he advised. "Who knows what might be inside."

However, there was nothing to harm them in the brick-walled room attached to the tower. In fact, there was nothing but mounds of earth covering the floor and partially barring the entrance to still another room alongside.

Quickly scaling that mound of earth, Sue slid down the other side into the second room. Roy was right behind her, and they scrutinized the interior revealed by the beam from his battery lantern.

"Not even a nail," came Roy's dejected call to the

three teenagers waiting in the other room. "Don't even bother to come in here." And he climbed back over the mound of dirt in the doorway.

"Sure looks like somebody did a lot of digging here," Sue commented, after they had examined some of the piles of dirt littering the floor.

Roy nodded. "I guess the Army did that when they were removing whatever equipment they had in here."

Both Chad and Alana looked doubtful, but they offered no argument as Roy went over to what looked like a window in the west wall. Actually the "window" was another doorway leading to the outside. It only looked like a window because of the dirt that had been piled in front of it.

Once outside, Alana, Chad, Sue, and Andy stared around them in amazement. A few feet from the doorway they had just come through, another wall extended into the woods to the west.

Only Roy, who had unfolded Sue's map and was looking at it, did not register any surprise. "Except for the tower and the tunnel in back of us," he said, "this looks just like that first target wall we walked along." And Roy gestured toward the wall on their left, then down at the concrete walk which ran parallel to the base of the wall.

"If I'm reading this map correctly," Roy went on, "there'll be another tunnel at the end of this wall."

Andy's gray eyes surveyed the wall looming high above them. "We're not going to walk up there, are we?"

Roy shook his head. "The wall must be at least twenty feet high at this point, and there's no way we could climb up there without ropes."

"I'm glad of that," Andy said with a sigh of relief. "I like my feet on solid ground!"

"Me too!" Sue chimed in, for once agreeing with her brother as she skipped down the concrete walkway toward the second tunnel.

Similar to the first tunnel, the one they now entered ran from north to south, with long narrow ventilation slits in the west wall. The east wall was blank, except for another shallow metal box which Roy discovered about midway through the tunnel. This box was totally empty—not even a spider had found its rusted interior inviting enough to spin a web. Nor did their flashlights reveal anything else of interest throughout the whole length of the tunnel. It was as empty as the first.

There was one difference, though. As they neared the end of the tunnel, the five explorers found that a section of the roof had caved in, leaving a pile of rubble to block any further progress in that direction. However, there was a doorway in the west wall which led to the outside.

"No more towers?" Andy asked as they stood outside

looking up at still another wall leading off to the west.

"The map shows only one tower," Roy confirmed, his dark hair falling into his eyes as he bent over the sketch Sue had made.

"But that wall over there leads to another tunnel, correct?" Andy questioned.

"Nope," Roy told him. "The pattern of walls and tunnels changes here. According to Sue's map, the tunnel we were just in continues in a straight line in the same direction—south—except that it's blocked by rubble from where the roof caved in. Meanwhile, this wall continues west until it meets another short wall."

Chad had been staring over Roy's shoulder at the map. His long index finger pointing to the place where the two walls met at right angles, he murmured, "There must be a reason why those walls were built that way."

"Why don't we go find out?" Sue spoke up.

"I'm game," Andy said, "as long as we don't have to walk on top of the wall."

"The ground slopes up by the tunnel," Roy pointed out, "so the wall isn't so high right here. It'll be easy to get on top of it, and it'll certainly be better walking up there than bushwhacking through the woods. Or haven't you noticed, Andy, there's no concrete walkway alongside this wall?"

Defeated by Roy's logic, Andy shrugged his compli-

76

ance, and followed the others as they climbed to the top of the wall.

For some reason, this wall was in poorer condition than the other two they had encountered. To make matters worse, the wall was also narrower, and the five had to concentrate on keeping their balance as they stepped over and around the cracks in the crumbling cement. Fortunately this third wall was much shorter than the two others, so it took no more than five minutes for them to reach the spot where the wall made a sharp right turn to the north, then ended abruptly.

"Another great big nothing," Andy muttered, mopping his perspiring face.

"Not quite," Alana corrected cheerily, even though she, too, was fatigued from the noontime heat. Pointing to where a small stream could be seen through the trees beyond the wall, she added, "Why don't we have our lunch over there where it will be cooler?" Then without waiting for their agreement, she climbed down from the wall and set off through the trees.

The others eagerly scrambled after her, voicing their approval when they discovered a large flat rock extending part way into the stream.

As they munched the somewhat soggy lettuce and tomato sandwiches Sue had supplied, they seemed to have forgotten their frightening experiences in the first tunnel and the tower, as well as the sinister stories Sue had told them about this long-abandoned Army camp. Totally relaxed, they lounged on the rock listening to the hum of the insects hovering over the slow-moving stream.

It was the ever-energized Sue who finally moved. Picking up some small flat stones, she began skipping them across the water. When she managed to get one to hop three times before it sank, Andy's competitive spirit was stirred and he started skipping stones too. Before long, Alana and Chad had joined in and all four scrambled along the stream bank, laughing and joking as they searched for the thin flat rocks that made the best skipping stones.

Roy, however, had remained seated on the large rock, a frown drawing his thick black eyebrows together as he rubbed his right knee. Noticing this, Sue gathered up some skipping stones and brought them over to him.

"Here, Roy," she offered. "Join in the fun."

"Nah!" came his irritable reply. "I'm sixteen—not six!"

A hurt expression was evident in Sue's eyes as well as in her voice when she said, "Well, here're some pebbles anyway—just in case you change your mind."

Roy did change his mind—and immediately. Picking

up a few of the pebbles, he glanced down at them as if too ashamed of himself to look into Sue's troubled gray eyes. "I'm sorry, Peanut," he mumbled. "I didn't mean to snap at you."

"I know, Roy," she answered slowly. "I know your knee is bothering you." Then Sue grinned. "But even my Dad likes to skip stones across a stream. And he's forty years old—not sixteen or even six!"

The smile that had begun to spread over Roy's face abruptly turned into a frown, and Sue looked as if she regretted her last sentence. Then she realized Roy's frown was not one of anger but of concentration as he studied the pebbles still in his palm.

"What is it, Roy?" Sue asked.

Picking out a triangular piece of white rock, Roy held it up for Sue to see. "Look at the edges, Sue," he urged. "Look at the point."

Roy's excitement was infectious, and Sue could only stutter, "That's . . . that's . . ."

"An arrowhead!" Alana cried out as she joined them on the flat rock. "I don't know exactly what type of point it is—my father could tell you about that. But he taught me enough to recognize an arrowhead when I see one."

"And where there's one, there may be more!" Sue whooped. Sliding off the rock, she began clawing through the pebbles along the stream bank. She was not alone either, for Andy, Alana, and Chad were just as enthusiastically searching the water's edge.

Although they searched for half an hour in the vicinity of the flat rock, they did not find any more arrowheads, which prompted Roy to say, "No sense in killing ourselves looking. That arrowhead we found could have been washed down by the stream from anywhere."

"Maybe," Alana answered, "but if Indians lived here . . ."

"And they did!" Sue broke in.

"Then they'd have left behind some more evidence of their being here," Alana finished. Pointing upstream toward a place where a large mound of dirt rose up from the otherwise level area by the water's edge, Alana went on, "That looks interesting. What say we . . ."

"What say we finish exploring the artillery range?" Roy interrupted. "That's what we're here for, aren't we?"

The irritation had returned to his voice, but Sue didn't seem to notice it as she said, "I'm so glad we found something—something you can write about in a term paper for Miss Stitt's history class, Roy."

With a brusque gesture, Roy handed the arrowhead back to Sue. "Did you forget? I won't be writing any paper because I won't be going back to school. Nothing has changed my mind about that!"

80

Stunned by the vehemence of Roy's words, his four companions could only stare at him as he headed back toward the wall.

"Roy's head is as hard as the quartz in that arrowhead we found," Chad muttered in disgust.

Alana nodded, her lips drawn into a thin, tight line.

Sue, however, was not so glum. Holding up the arrowhead, she studied it a moment, then said, "Take a look at the way this arrowhead was made." Then she pointed it at the retreating Roy. "This piece of quartz may be hard just like Roy's head," she went on, "but the Indians managed to shape it just the way they wanted it. And maybe if we use their method, we can do the same with Roy."

Andy let out one of the exasperated snorts he saved just for his sister's remarks. "Is that some kind of riddle, Sue?"

Just then Chad laughed, "Oh, I get it." Then turning to the baffled Andy, he explained, "Indians made arrowheads by chipping off bits of rock a little at a time. So what Sue's saying is that we've got to have the same kind of patience and persistence the Indians had."

"That's it exactly!" Sue declared. "We've just got to keep chipping away at Roy, and maybe in time we can change his mind."

Andy nodded that he finally understood. But his

tone was far from optimistic when he said, "I hope you're right, Sue. And I also hope you don't hurt yourself while you're chipping away."

Ahead of them, Roy continued to plod toward the wall.

"Wait up, Roy!" Alana called. "I'd like to see one more thing before we leave this section of Camp Gray Owl." Then turning to her companions, she said, "Let's try for one more chip."

10

At first Roy was reluctant to return to the stream bank. But Alana was persuasive and Roy could not deny that it would take only a few more minutes to reach the place Alana wanted to see. He even mustered up a little enthusiasm when Alana went on to explain she wanted to examine the mound they had spotted earlier because it did not look natural to her—that perhaps it was man-made.

"How could you possibly tell the difference from this distance?" Roy grunted.

"I'm an archaeologist's daughter, remember?" Alana answered.

"And remember the reason Chief Gray Owl refused to leave here!" Sue spoke up, as she followed the others across the stream by way of a series of conveniently placed stepping-stones.

The mound was about thirty feet long and twenty

feet wide, with one end almost submerged in the stream, while the other end pointed toward the north. And although a carpet of dying vegetation camouflaged what lay beneath, the large stones which protruded through the overlying layer of dirt and grass indicated that something more powerful than the slow-moving stream had piled up this large accumulation of rock.

"Maybe the mound is a glacial moraine," Andy commented, surprising everyone with his scientific terminology. "We learned about those things in school last year—large accumulations of rocks left behind when the glaciers melted. And there were plenty of glaciers here in the Northeast," he concluded.

Chad was shaking his head. So was Roy. "Nope," they both said at the same time.

"Too small," Chad added.

"Too perfectly shaped," was Roy's reason.

"Then what could it be?" Andy wanted to know.

Sue raised her voice above the others. "I told you what it was before, only you didn't listen. Remember the story about Chief Gray Owl? He wouldn't leave here because his people were buried here—in mounds!"

Alana's blue eyes quickly traveled to the highest point of the mound, about ten feet above the surrounding ground. Then her gaze swung down over the rounded sides. "It does look like some of the mounds I saw when my father took me with him on one of his digs down South," she murmured. "Only it's smaller. And from what my father has said, I don't think Northeastern Indians buried their dead like that."

"But doesn't your father also say that not enough is known about the archaeology of the Northeast?" Roy spoke up. "Chad wasn't the only one who took that course in amateur archaeology that your Dad taught last year. I did too. And I remember him saying that a lot more study has to be done of the Northeast, especially of stone structures like this."

Sue had been jumping up and down as Roy was speaking. "That's what you should do, Roy!" she sang out. "When you go to college, you should major in archaeology so you can explore these things when you graduate!"

Before Roy could snap out any angry answer, Chad stepped forward. "That Indian mound stuff is probably just a silly legend," he said.

Alana's eyebrows had shot up at this uncharacteristic remark of Chad's, but she said nothing. Roy said it for her.

"The legend could be true!" the black-haired boy declared emphatically.

"It's much more likely some Army bulldozer just piled up a load of rocks here," Chad went on.

Roy scowled. "You're wrong about that!"

"Prove it!" Chad challenged.

"I will!" Roy roared back, taken in by Chad's deliberate attempt to bait him. "I sure will prove it—maybe not today, but someday!"

If he realized that the other four had developed grins of satisfaction, Roy was too worked up to consider why they might be smiling that way, or why Chad had said what he did. "Let me just show you something for now," Roy continued, as he bent over to dislodge one of the stones protruding from the mound. "See how carefully these stones seem to have been placed? They look as if . . ."

A shrill scream from Sue cut off whatever it was Roy had intended to say.

"Snakes!" Sue screamed again. "There's snakes coming out of the mound!"

Something long and black slithered past Roy's kneeling form, and disappeared in the grass. Another serpentine body followed the first one, almost touching Roy's hands still holding the rock he had dislodged.

For a moment, he remained frozen in position. Then he jerked upright, his eyes still on the hole from which the snakes had emerged.

"Run, Roy!" Sue called from the opposite bank of the shallow stream she had already plunged across. "Run!"

The others had done exactly as Sue, and all were now racing away from the stream, heading toward the safety of the wall. Even Chad panicked momentarily, and apparently he did not even think of the friend he had left behind until he had almost reached the wall. Then Chad's reasoning power took over, and he halted his headlong flight.

Chad turned around just in time to see Roy sprawl headfirst.

"The snake's got him!" Sue screamed. "Roy's been bitten by the snake!"

This time Chad didn't panic. Reaching down for a stout tree limb that was lying on the ground, he quickly made his way to where Roy had fallen. Using the tree limb as a club, Chad beat on the ground around Roy's body.

"What are you trying to do, finish me off?" came Roy's half-joking, half-serious question.

"I'm trying to scare off that snake," Chad panted. "Where did it bite you?"

"What snake? What bite?" By now, Roy was sitting up and holding his right leg.

"You weren't bitten?" Chad asked.

"Boy, we're really some outdoorsmen!" Roy declared. "Maybe the other three wouldn't have known, but you and I should have realized those snakes were trying to get away from us—not chase us. They're probably still on the other side of the stream, going as fast as they can in the opposite direction!"

"But if you weren't bitten, then why . . ."

"Because I tripped over that bramble bush!" Roy answered through lips twisted in pain. "And now I think I've hurt my leg again."

Happily, Roy was wrong. His knee had not been reinjured by the fall. It was only a skinned shin which was causing his pain. He was soon able to walk without any help from Chad, and they joined the other three on the wall.

For long minutes the five young people silently sat there, eyeing each other sheepishly, each one reluctant to bring up the subject of their panic. Alana, Andy, and Sue had overheard what Roy said about the snakes, and they shifted around uncomfortably on the rough concrete wall. Finally it was Alana who spoke.

"I think Camp Gray Owl is getting to us," she said. "Talk about losing your head, we sure did that just now."

"It's all those scary stories Sue told us," Andy maintained.

"I didn't make them up!" Sue protested.

"I didn't say you did," Andy retorted. "It's just that stories like that—ghosts and curses and artillery shells that didn't land where they were supposed to— well, it's enough to make you think snakes are chasing you even when they aren't."

Sue frowned thoughtfully. "But what if this place

really is cursed?" she addressed the others. Then turning back to her brother, she added, "Even you, Andy, have to admit some mighty weird things have been happening to us here."

The boy let out his familiar snort. "You mean weird things like a common old mole running down a tunnel behind you?"

"That's only your version of what happened yesterday!" Sue shot back. "But if you don't think that was unusual, how about the owl that hoots in the daytime instead of at night like he's supposed to?"

"Just a crazy mixed-up bird, like a certain relative of mine who . . ."

"Cease firing!" Chad ordered. "Those verbal bullets of yours are worse than any of Camp Gray Owl's misdirected artillery shells! And speaking of Camp Gray Owl, don't you think we should continue our explorations? Remember that third tunnel on the other side of the target wall?"

"How do you expect to explore that third tunnel?" Alana wanted to know. "Wasn't it blocked?"

Chad shrugged. "Maybe we can crawl over the rubble to get on the other side. It's worth a try anyway."

It took only a few minutes for them to retrace their steps to where the third target wall joined the second tunnel. While his companions waited, Chad climbed down and reentered the doorway of the second tunnel in order to examine the pile of concrete chunks from the caved-in roof. The mound seemed stable enough, so he carefully climbed up the side, eventually emerging through the hole in the roof of the tunnel.

"I should have gone this way to start with," he told the four others who were sitting on the target wall only a few feet from where he climbed out.

Flopping down next to them on the wall, Chad went on, "All we have to do is to crawl down the slope of the rubble on the north side to get into the second tunnel, or crawl down the south slope of the rubble to enter the other tunnel."

Roy shook his head. "I think I'm going to sit this one out," he told Chad.

"You're not giving up, are you, Roy?" Sue cried.

"I'm not giving up, Peanut," the dark-haired boy assured her. "It's just that I think I'd better give this banged-up leg a few minutes' rest. Plus that, I'd like to have another look at this map."

"Maybe that would be best," Chad agreed. "That other tunnel does look like it's in pretty bad shape, Roy. So there's no sense in all of us going down in there only to have to turn around and come right back here."

"In that case, I think I'll rest awhile too," Alana said.

"And I'll keep Roy company," Sue offered.

90

Turning to Andy, Chad asked, "Are you still game?"

"Yup!" Andy said, then added with a wink, "I'd do anything to get away from Sue's chatter!" And he scooted over to the hole in the tunnel roof before his sister could deliver the poke in the ribs she had aimed at him.

Chad had already lowered himself part way into the hole, but he paused when Alana called softly, "Be careful, Chad."

"Don't worry," he called back. "See you all in a little while." Then he disappeared into the tunnel with Andy right behind him.

"But you *are* worried, aren't you?" Roy asked when Alana sat back down beside him.

Her long blonde hair brushing against her cheeks as she nodded, Alana said slowly, "Ever since we got here today, I've felt as if someone or something has been watching us. I had the same feeling yesterday too. But we haven't seen anyone, have we?"

"Nope," the younger girl agreed cheerfully. "Not even the ghost of old Gray Owl!" But Sue's attempt at humor fell flat, and for some reason all three of them shuddered.

11

The Third Tunnel

Dark, dank, damp—the third tunnel was all of that and more. It was dangerous as well. For unlike the other two tunnels with their sturdy concrete corridors, deep cracks ran along the walls and ceiling of the third tunnel, causing Andy to gasp when he saw them.

"It . . . it looks like pictures of houses after an earthquake has struck!" he exclaimed.

"Or after a couple of artillery shells struck," Chad reasoned.

"But didn't we figure out that these tunnels run north to south?" Andy asked. "And that because they were parallel to the line of fire they wouldn't have been hit by the artillery shells?"

Chad nodded. "That's true, but aren't you forgetting the reason the Army closed down the place?"

"Oh," Andy said with a grin. "The shells that didn't land in the right places. I guess this tunnel must have been one of the wrong places."

"Sure looks like it," Chad agreed as he began stepping over the chunks of rock and concrete that littered the floor.

Andy hurried forward to place a restraining hand on his friend's arm. "Do you think we ought to go on? Do you think it's safe?"

Chad once again swung his battery lantern in a wide arc. "Oh, I think so," he answered after a few moments. "Just as long as we're careful."

"Well, okay," came Andy's less than enthusiastic reply. "But what makes it so dark in here? The other tunnels at least had some light coming through the ventilation slits."

Chad shrugged. "When we were sitting on the target wall just before we came in here, I noticed a lot of trees and bushes growing along that side of the tunnel. They're probably blocking the light from coming through the ventilation slits. Then, too, some of the slits could be filled with debris. But it really doesn't matter, because I see light ahead. Maybe it's another hole in the roof."

If it were not so dark within the crumbling tunnel, Andy might not have paid particular attention to the shaft of light coming in through a large crack in the east wall. As it was, the jagged scar in the otherwise windowless wall on the left side of the tunnel just ahead of him drew Andy's gaze, and his eyes remained focused on it as he and Chad approached the crack.

"Wouldn't it be nice if we could find some shell casings?" Andy mused. "There might be some around here if it was artillery fire that damaged this . . ."

Breaking off his sentence, Andy stopped walking and stared at the light-filled crack a few feet farther along the tunnel. "Did you see that, Chad? Did you?" he almost shouted.

"See what?" Chad asked, looking up from his study of the tunnel floor.

"The shadow that passed across the shaft of light coming in through the crack in the wall!" Andy breathlessly explained.

"You mean something's here in the tunnel?" Chad asked, as he raised the battery lantern to illuminate the corridor ahead of them.

"No! No!" Andy told him. "It was more like something moving outside. Something that interrupted the light from coming in through that crack."

Both boys rushed over to the jagged crack in the thick tunnel wall. Though it zigzagged all the way from the ceiling almost to the floor, it was only about five inches at its widest point—not enough for them to stick their heads through, nor even for them to see much of the outside, except for what was directly in front of the crack. And the only thing which greeted their eyes was a tangled mass of vegetation.

"Something did move out there!" Andy insisted. "It passed right by this crack."

"The shadow could have been caused by a tree moving in the wind."

"There is no wind today," Andy pointed out.

"Or the sun behind a cloud . . ."

"There are no clouds."

"Then maybe . . . maybe you only thought you saw a shadow," Chad concluded. "You know how places like this can work on your imagination."

Andy sighed in resignation. "Maybe you're right, Chad." But he added with a forlorn tone, "Now I know what Sue felt like when we didn't believe her tunnel story."

Chad chuckled. "Cheer up, Andy. As the old saying goes, 'There's light at the end of the tunnel.' And there really is—at least at what seems to be the end of the tunnel for us."

About twenty yards ahead of them they could see light filtering down through another hole in the roof of the tunnel—a hole that was almost completely filled by the trunk of a tree whose many roots were firmly entwined in a mound of rubble on the tunnel floor.

"Now what tree in its right mind would try to grow in a spot like that?" Andy asked in amazement.

"I don't think the seed had any choice in the matter," Chad laughed. "And neither do we." He pointed to

95

a huge slab of concrete that had once been part of the roof but was now standing on end. It, along with the tree, effectively blocked the passage.

"I see what you mean," Andy said without the slightest bit of disappointment. "We can't go any farther, so we'll have to go back the way we came."

The return trip through the debris-littered tunnel was uneventful, except for a brief moment when Chad snagged one of his bootlaces on a projecting sliver of rock. But he was able to recover his balance without falling, and a few minutes later he and Andy were climbing back through the hole in the tunnel roof near the target wall.

"Any luck?" Sue called out the minute she spotted them.

Without going over to where the three others were seated on the target wall, Chad answered, "The tunnel is blocked by a cave-in not far from here, and the whole thing's in pretty bad shape."

"No art-tracks, either," Andy chimed in, winking at his sister, who only frowned at him in reply.

"So where do we go from here?" Alana asked. "Roy's been looking at the map, and it seems there're still more walls at the southern end of the tunnel."

Chad nodded. "Andy and I will go take a look, okay?"

"Why don't we all go?" Sue wanted to know. "We'd

like to see the rest of this place too."

"I didn't mean that Andy and I should explore the rest of Camp Gray Owl alone," Chad explained. "Just that Andy and I find out whether it would be better to walk on top of the third tunnel, or maybe get down on the solid ground and go along by the side of the west wall. The land is fairly level on that side, but it begins sloping down steeply along the east wall of the tunnel."

"Wouldn't we be able to see more if we stayed on top of the tunnel?" Roy questioned.

Chad pointed to where the tunnel roof had caved in. "This isn't the only hole in the top of the tunnel. There's another one farther down, and there may be others that would prevent us from continuing along the top. That's why I suggested Andy and I check it out first."

"Right-o. Good thinking, chap!" Sue sang out in imitation of a British Army officer she had seen in a World War II movie on TV the night before.

The laughter that greeted Sue's impersonation followed Chad and Andy as they set off along the top of the third tunnel, heading south. But even with the sounds of merriment filling the air, Chad did not fail to hear Alana call, "Do be careful, Chad. It could be dangerous . . ."

12

◁——————*An Unseen Hand*

Chad and Andy needed no reminder to be cautious. The cracked and crumbling concrete beneath their feet was warning enough. So they proceeded carefully along the top of the third tunnel until they got to the place where the tree was growing through the hole made when the roof had caved in.

Only a narrow strip of concrete remained on either side of the hole to connect the north end of the tunnel wall with the southern section.

"I wouldn't trust that bit of concrete," Chad warned Andy, who already had one foot on the narrow strip at the western side of the hole. "Hang on to the tree. It seems sturdy enough."

The tree was sturdy, all right. The concrete strip was not. As soon as Andy's full weight was upon it, several inches gave way, and a cloud of concrete particles went tumbling down the cracked western side of the tunnel wall. Andy, however, had been prepared. Holding on to the tree, he easily swung his weight past the unstable strip and landed on the solid southern section of the tunnel.

"You know, we could get into the rest of the tunnel from this side," he called over to Chad. "It's like the hole back there near the target wall."

Chad's answer was a grunt.

"What's wrong?" Andy asked, peering around the branches of the tree to see his friend on one knee on the northern side of the hole.

"My bootlace is broken," Chad explained. "Give me a minute to fix it, and I'll come over there for a look-see. But I think we'd do better to stay out of the tunnel and continue along the top of the wall—that is, if it isn't completely crumbled down farther on."

"Not as far as I can see, but I can't see too much because of the trees overlapping . . . Hey, there're some more walls up ahead, Chad."

"Be with you in just a minute," Chad answered.

"Hurry up," Andy urged.

"I'm trying to," Chad said, "but the lace broke halfway down the boot. I've got to unlace it to that point, then tie it, then lace it back up."

"I thought all good mountain climbers check to see

their bootlaces are okay before starting out on a trip,"
Andy teased, but there was a note of impatience in
his voice.

"I put in new laces yesterday," Chad replied calmly.
"This must have happened when my boot got caught
on that sliver of rock down in the tunnel. I'll only be
a little while longer. But I want to make sure this
lace is secure when I try squeezing past that tree."

"I know what you mean," Andy agreed, but he was
still restlessly shifting from one foot to the other. "I
might as well go on ahead and check on those walls,"
he added after a short pause. "You can catch up when
you're finished, Chad."

Still working with the defective lace, Chad frowned.
"Andy, I don't think . . ." Then hearing the sound
of his friend's fading footsteps, Chad stopped long
enough to gaze around the branches of the tree growing
out of the hole. But there were still more branches
from other trees rooted next to the western side of
the wall. These branches overlapped the top of the
tunnel only a few yards south of the hole, and when
Chad looked, Andy was already out of sight.

"Hard head!" Chad muttered as he redoubled his
efforts to secure the bootlace. Once this was done, he
straightened up and approached the narrow strip of
concrete which bordered the eastern side of the hole.

The cracked concrete seemed as untrustworthy as

that which Andy had encountered on the western edge of the hole, and Chad took careful hold of the tree. As he did so, he glanced over the edge of the tunnel wall, and what he saw below gave him a queasy feeling. Chad had observed earlier that, unlike the fairly level land adjoining the western wall of the tunnel, the eastern side fell away sharply, as if the tunnel had been built along the edge of a small cliff—a cliff at whose base lay a jumbled mass of sharp-edged rocks.

As he glanced down at those rocks thirty feet below him, Chad said to himself, "Maybe I'd better try to get past this tree on the other side, like Andy did."

But worry about his friend had diluted his usual caution. And muttering something about "Andy shouldn't have gone on ahead like that," Chad proceeded to skirt the tree by way of the narrow concrete strip on the western edge of the tunnel top.

Hurry can make anyone careless, and Chad was no exception. Facing the tree, he began moving sideways along the concrete strip. Midway, he was forced to lean back to avoid one thick branch, and he stepped too quickly. Just as quickly he felt the sole of his boot slide on a patch of lichen growing in one of the small cracks in the concrete.

It was a slip of only a few inches, but that was enough to make Chad lose his balance and his grip on the tree. In one gulping moment of terror, he felt himself hurtling downward—down to the sharp rocks below.

Instinct more than reason was what saved him. Without consciously knowing that he did so, Chad frantically swung his arms as he plummeted downward, clawing wildly for something to hold on to. And then he touched it—a slim but solid branch of the tree.

As any plant will do, the tree had sought the life-giving sunlight outside the dim tunnel where its seed had taken root. Growing up through the hole in the tunnel roof, it had also pushed branches out through the crack in the eastern side of the wall. It was one of those branches that Chad's right hand encountered, and his descent was brought to a jolting, wrist-numbing stop.

For one sickening second he hung there by one hand, his whole arm seared by the pain of his effort. Then Chad's other arm swung up to bring his left hand in contact with the branch. Finally his fingers closed around it, bringing some relief to his agonized right hand.

"Whew! That was a close one!" Chad gasped. But his satisfaction at having saved himself was short-lived, for it immediately became apparent that he was far from safe.

A fast look overhead, then below him, revealed to Chad that he had fallen about a third of the way down the side of the hill. The base of the tunnel was almost at eye level, and Chad shuddered when he saw that he had grabbed on to the very lowest—and last—branch growing out from the crack in the tunnel's eastern wall. Below that the almost perpendicular side of the hill descended another twenty feet—too great a distance to risk letting go and landing on the pointed rocks below.

He had only two choices, Chad decided as he hung there, fingernails digging into the rough bark of the tree limb. He could try to reach the side of the hill by going hand over hand along the length of the branch, or he could try swinging his legs up to wrap around the branch and proceed from there.

The first thought was quickly discarded when Chad realized his waning strength was not enough to allow him to transfer his weight from hand to hand as he moved along the branch. What's more, the numerous smaller branches growing out from the main limb would make progress almost impossible.

The only answer was to keep holding on with both hands, meanwhile swinging his body back and forth like a pendulum. When he had gained enough momentum on one of the upward swings, he would be able to reach up with his legs and wrap them around the branch. But would his aching arms withstand the added strain caused by his pendulum-like movements? What's more, was the branch itself strong enough?

103

The silent questions seared through his brain as Chad emitted a strangled shout:

"Andy! Andy, I need help! Andy, hurry!"

But even as his cry sliced through the afternoon stillness, Chad realized the foolishness of waiting for help to reach him—that is, if Andy had even heard his call. Already the muscles in his forearms were twitching from the unrelieved strain, and his wrists and shoulders felt as if they had been dislocated. If he didn't act now, it would be too late.

Drops of salty sweat dripped into his eyes, and Chad turned his head to wipe his face against the damp fabric covering his tortured, upraised shoulders. Clenching his jaw, he concentrated on the extra effort he must demand of his already overburdened arms.

Something like an electric current—excruciating and numbing at the same time—surged through his wrists and shoulders as Chad began his first swing. He gasped, but continued the forward and backward motion, trying to lift his legs on the upward swing in order to get them around the branch.

On the fourth swing, Chad almost lost his grip on the tree limb. A sharp twig was biting into the palm of his right hand, and the added pain made the effort unbearable. Plus that, the branch creaked ominously with every movement of his body. If the limb of the tree broke off . . .

104

Panting heavily, Chad ceased his movements, wondering how much longer he would be able to hang on to the branch even if he remained motionless.

"Andy! Andy, come help me . . . please . . ." Chad's last word was more of a sob than a shout, and when its echo died away he lowered his head, fighting back a feeling of helplessness and hopelessness.

There had been no answering shout from Andy—not to Chad's first call, nor to the one he had just emitted, and Chad could only conclude that his impetuous friend had gone too far ahead to hear his cry.

"Andy! Roy! Anyone—help!"

The forlorn voice was weaker now, as were his quivering arms, and Chad knew it would be only a matter of moments before he would have to let go. No amount of concentration, no exertion of willpower could prevent that. The exhausted muscles would simply give up on their own.

Then it happened.

Where earlier his booted feet had been dangling in empty space, suddenly Chad felt something solid under the sole of his right foot.

Was it some lower tree branch he hadn't seen? A projecting ledge of rock?

But there was not time to answer these questions, for whatever it was under his foot was exerting pressure—pressure upward—and Chad found himself automatically swinging his left leg up to straddle the tree branch.

From there Chad frantically reached for the next limb a few feet above the one he had been hanging from only a few seconds earlier. Standing on the second limb, his quivering arms could reach the top of the tunnel roof. But by then, other stronger arms were reaching down to help him, and the exhausted Chad was soon pulled up to the tunnel roof by Andy.

"What happened? Did you fall? Did you hurt yourself?"

Waving a weary hand to indicate he would answer Andy's questions as soon as he regained his breath, Chad sprawled out on the tunnel roof. But Andy was unable to remain quiet.

"Did the concrete give way? How far did you drop? And how did you get back up?"

Andy's last question jolted Chad to a sitting position. Narrowing his eyes in remembrance, he stared at Andy for just a moment. Then Chad shifted sideways, getting on his hands and knees to peer down over the eastern side of the wall.

Meanwhile, Andy's excited voice continued, "I heard you call for help and I started back. But the top of the tunnel's in pretty bad shape farther along, with lots of trees growing beside . . ." Andy's words died away when he realized Chad's attention was elsewhere.

"What's so interesting down there?" Andy asked, kneeling down to look over the edge of the tunnel wall.

"Yes, what is it you're looking for?" came Roy's voice as the three others hurriedly approached the kneeling boys.

"We thought we heard a call for help," Sue said as she joined Chad and Andy, still gazing down at the rocks below the wall. "What do you see?"

With a puzzled frown on his face, Chad raised his head. "That's the problem. I don't see anything at all!"

Misinterpreting what Chad meant, Sue asked with concern, "You mean something happened to your eyes, Chad? You mean you can't see those jagged rocks down there or . . ."

"No, no," Chad broke in. "I can see all of that. What I meant is I can't see whatever it was that helped me climb back up."

From the blank expressions on his friends' faces, Chad realized he had better explain what had happened to him from the time Andy had left him by the tree growing out of the hole in the tunnel roof. This he did quickly and quietly, ending by saying, "So I still can't figure out how I got up here. When I felt that thing under my foot, I didn't even look down. All I was thinking about was reaching the top."

107

"Maybe there was another branch of the tree—one you weren't able to see when you were hanging from the other one. Maybe you happened to put your foot on it, and . . ." Roy didn't complete his sentence because Chad was shaking his head from side to side.

"That's what I was looking for when you three arrived," Chad told his friends. "But there's no branch, no rock near enough—not anything I could have put my foot on. Anyway, neither of those things would explain the boost upwards that I felt."

Alana reached over to place her hand on Chad's sweat-dampened back. "Maybe you only thought you felt something push on your foot. You know how . . ."

Again Chad shook his head. "I know what I felt," he insisted. "And I know something—or someone— gave me a boost up!"

Uneasy glances were exchanged.

"You . . . you mean something like a . . . a ghost?" Sue asked fearfully.

"Well, it sure was something I couldn't see," Chad replied. "At least whatever it was isn't visible down there now. But something did save me from falling on those rocks and possibly breaking my neck. So if it's a ghost, it must be a good ghost—definitely not the vengeful haunt of Chief Gray Owl that you were telling us about, Sue."

Andy looked up with a tentative smile. But Chad's serious eyes made it obvious that he had not said this as a joke, and the smile faded from Andy's lips.

"A good ghost," Sue said slowly. "Could there really be such a thing as a good ghost?"

13

◁——— *Only a Good Ghost . . .*

Despite the cheerful sunshine of the September afternoon, a gloomy mood had settled over the group as they sat on the tunnel roof, giving Chad a chance to recover from his recent ordeal.

Seeing Chad grimace as he flexed the fingers of his right hand, Alana suggested, "Maybe we better head for home. You've had enough for one day, Chad."

"Oh, I'm not so bad off," Chad assured her. "My fingers are just a little stiff from hanging on to that tree branch."

Roy looked up from his study of Sue's map. "There's no sense in pushing yourself, Chad. But if you really feel like staying a little longer . . ."

"Sure I do," Chad told him. "I want to see the rest of this place!"

Spirits lifted by Chad's enthusiastic reply, they began discussing their next move. From Andy's description of the rest of the tunnel roof, it was their unanimous decision not to continue along the crumbling top of the tunnel. Nor would they attempt an exploration of the inside of the tunnel, even though they would have been able to enter the southern section through that part of the hole on the other side of the tree.

"After all," Andy concluded, "if the top of the tunnel is in such bad condition, you can just imagine what it must be like inside!"

"So that's settled," Roy stated, as he folded Sue's map and stood up. "The only logical way is to bush-whack through the woods alongside the western wall of the tunnel."

Sue looked up quickly. "But didn't you say those other two walls are on the eastern side of the tunnel? How will we ever get to see them if we stay on the western side?"

Roy opened up the map once more and held it out to Sue. "Take a look," he said. "This tunnel extends only a little way past those two walls. All we'll have to do is walk around the southern end of the tunnel and we'll be able to see those walls—that is, if your map is accurate."

"It's accurate, all right!" Sue insisted. "I even put in those curly things on either side of the tunnel down by the two walls. See?" And she pointed out two pairs of short, curved lines, one pair on either side of the

111

longer lines representing the third tunnel.

"Curly things?" Andy asked with a laugh. "What kind of curly things?"

"How should I know?" Sue said in an exasperated tone of voice. "I just put down what I saw on the other map."

"And you put down everything you saw?" This time Roy was the questioner.

Sue stared up at him in surprise. "Of course I put down everything—at least I did until I ran out of paper."

"You mean there were more markings on the original map?" Roy asked immediately.

Sue shook her head. "Not really. There was just some old box or square in this corner of the other map, right about here." Sue pointed to a spot a couple of inches off the edge of the map Roy still held open. "I didn't put it down because I'd run out of paper, but it didn't look like anything anyway, and the word next to it was too blurred for me to copy it."

Roy's only comment was a low "Hmmmmm," as he folded up the map and once more put it in his pocket.

"Is something the matter, Roy?" Alana asked.

Roy shrugged. "It's just that I thought . . ."

"What?" Chad prompted when Roy's words trailed off.

"Oh, never mind," Roy replied. "Let's go find out what those curly things are."

Retracing their steps to where the tunnel met the target wall they had explored earlier, they were able to climb down and proceed south on the level ground bordering the western side of the tunnel wall. Even though the land was level, it was heavily wooded, with thick underbrush that tore at their clothing and impeded their pace.

"This is really something," Alana commented. She had paused to hold on to a thick vine so that it wouldn't snap back and hit Chad, who was right behind her.

"But the vines are not as bad as that over there," Chad told her, pointing to the tunnel wall a few yards to their left.

As Andy had warned them, the exterior of the tunnel became progressively worse the farther along they went. Parts of it were completely caved in, with gaping cracks in other places and debris clogging those ventilation slits that had not been destroyed. Trailing vines and other vegetation had taken root wherever enough dirt had accumulated in the cracked concrete so that the tunnel had the appearance of a ruin much older than it actually was.

"If it wasn't for those curly things we saw on the map," Chad went on, "I think I'd vote for an end to our explorations."

Panting from the heat and the exertion, Alana nodded. "It's rough all right, but it's even rougher on Sue." And Alana gestured up ahead to where the younger girl, because of her smaller stature and shorter legs, was having a more difficult time getting through the thick underbrush. "For her sake, as well as Roy's, I hope those curly things turn out to be something interesting."

The "curly things" were indeed interesting, but still not the kind of discovery the five explorers had hoped to make. For those curved lines on the map represented a set of steps descending under the western wall of the tunnel, and another set emerging on the eastern side, where two short parallel walls had been built at right angles to the tunnel.

"Well, at least this is different from the other walls and tunnels we've seen," Alana said when she emerged from the underpass which had been dug out of the earth beneath the tunnel floor.

"But why would the Army make a passageway beneath the tunnel here, when they didn't do it anywhere else in Camp Gray Owl?" Andy pondered out loud.

"I've got a hunch those two short walls on the other side of the tunnel might have been used for a pistol range," Roy said. "If that was their purpose, then the underpass would have been more convenient for the soldiers to get back and forth—I mean the soldiers

114

who were firing their handguns at the targets on the walls. Underpasses wouldn't have been needed at the other target walls since those were probably used for big guns being fired from a distance."

By this time, all five had climbed up the steps on the other side of the tunnel and were looking at a wall, about thirty feet in length, which stretched eastward from its attachment to the tunnel. The land here was as level as that on the western side of the tunnel, which caused Chad to comment wryly, "I should have waited to fall off the tunnel at this point."

Roy grinned, "I guess the land slopes down just beyond that short wall. Why don't we take a look?"

Without waiting to see if his companions were following him, Roy walked over to the end of the short wall.

"What's behind it, Roy?" Sue called.

"Just the other short wall," the dark-haired boy called over his shoulder. "There's also an opening to the tunnel between the two walls, but it's pretty well broken down."

In the few seconds it took for the others to reach the end of the first of the twin walls, Roy had already walked over to the other one.

"The ground slopes down behind there," Roy reported as he came back. "And that's it."

"You mean that's all there is to Camp Gray Owl?" Sue asked disappointedly.

115

"That's all except for the ghosts," Roy said with a wink.

But Sue did not smile at his joke, and neither did Alana, who was eyeing the dark opening between the twin walls. "Well, if that's all there is," the blonde-haired girl began, "why don't we get out of this creepy place?"

"Camp Gray Owl still bothers you, doesn't it?" Chad asked sympathetically.

Alana nodded sheepishly.

"Aw, Alana, there's no such thing as ghosts," Andy declared. "My sister may be silly enough to believe in such things, but you should know better!"

"Better?" Alana echoed. "I'm not so sure I do know better," Alana went on. "All I know is that some funny things have been happening to us since we started exploring Camp Gray Owl."

Alana's words caused Chad to frown thoughtfully. Taking Alana's hand in his as they walked back to the steps leading under the tunnel, Chad said, "Everything that happened to us could have a logical explanation. It's only our imagination that makes it seem as if there's something supernatural about the place."

"But what about the boost up you got when you fell from the top of the tunnel?" Sue reminded Chad. "You were positive it wasn't your imagination."

Chad did not answer for several seconds, and when

116

he finally did it was to stutter feebly,"Well . . . uh . . . I . . . maybe . . ."

"Maybe what?" Sue pressed, as they climbed the last of the steps on the western side of the tunnel.

The brief moment it had taken Sue to say this had given Chad time to collect his thoughts. "Well, like I said before, if I was helped by a ghost, it could only have been a good ghost." Then as they emerged from the underpass, Chad added, "And there's no need to worry about good ghosts, is there?"

"But you haven't really answered . . ." Sue began, only to be cut off by Roy.

"Ghost or no ghost," he broke in, "we're not yet done with Camp Gray Owl. Just look what's up ahead through the trees!"

14

◁——*Command Post Treasure*

Following the direction in which Roy's finger was
pointing, the eyes of the other four focused on a house
almost totally hidden by the dense foliage. Only its
twin chimneys were apparent at this distance, and only
because those chimneys were constructed of a reddish
brick which contrasted with the surrounding shades
of leafy green that camouflaged the rest of the house.

"That's it!" Roy exclaimed excitedly. "I knew there
had to be one!"

Confronted with the bewildered glances of his companions, Roy quickly explained, "I felt there had to
be some sort of a command post—a place where the
Army brass would gather to plan and direct the opera-
tions. A command post would naturally be built in a
safe place—somewhere away from the actual firing.
But I couldn't find anything on the map that looked

118

like such a place, and I was about to give up until . . ."

"Until Sue mentioned the box she didn't have room for on her map!" Andy shouted.

"That's right," Roy confirmed. "That convinced me there had to be at least one more building in this part of the camp. But I didn't spot those chimneys until we came back out of the underpass."

By now, Sue was jumping up and down. "A command post—wow! There'll be something there for us to find. I just know there will!"

Brown ponytail bouncing, Sue plunged into the underbrush, heading straight for the tree-shrouded building several hundred yards to the southwest.

"Wait up!" Roy shouted. "We don't know for sure that's the command post."

"And we don't know what—or who—might be inside it!" Alana cried out.

Sue's checkered shirt had already disappeared behind the vine-entwined trunk of a massive maple tree, but it reappeared almost immediately following Alana's distraught call.

"You're right," the younger girl said contritely as she returned to where the other four were standing. "I guess I'm just anxious to see that house."

"We all are," Roy told her with a wide grin. Then

his face became serious. "But we've got to be cautious too."

Suiting actions to words, Roy gestured for his companions to follow him in single file as he carefully made his way through the underbrush toward the house with the red brick chimneys. Halfway there, he discovered a vague path that made the going easier as well as faster, and five minutes later they emerged from the woods in front of a two-story frame house.

Decades of disuse were evident in the warped wood siding that had weathered to a pewter-colored gray. Yet other boards, especially those which had been nailed over the window openings, still retained their original brownish hue. This prompted Chad's low-voiced speculation: "Looks like somebody's been here since the Army left."

"Hunters might use it," Roy ventured.

"Or hoboes," was Andy's suggestion.

"Or ghosts."

Sue's reference to the supernatural brought a loud guffaw from her brother. "Ghosts nailing boards up over windows?" Andy laughed. "Really, Sue, I've heard of carpenter ants, but never carpenter ghosts!"

Even Sue had to smile at Andy's remark and it was without fear that they began calling out to whoever might be inside. Receiving no answer, they decided the place was as deserted as the rest of Camp Gray

Owl, and they circled the house, looking for a way to get inside. When they finally found one—a back door on which a rusted padlock hung by its unengaged hook—Sue was jubilant.

Alana was not. "Do you really think we should go in there?" she asked nervously.

"I didn't see any posted signs, so we're certainly not trespassing," Roy replied.

"This is supposed to be public land, isn't it?" Andy pointed out.

"It sure is," Sue confirmed. "And we're not breaking into the house either, 'cause the door is unlocked."

Alana looked over at Chad, but he only shrugged noncommittally. "Well, maybe it is okay," Alana conceded.

Equally as gloomy as the tunnels had been, the interior of the house had a musty smell that irritated the nostrils of the five friends as they rummaged around in their knapsacks and backpacks for the flashlights they had used earlier.

The strong beam of Chad's battery lantern was the first to be turned on, and they all gasped at what it revealed.

Lined up in perfect order on a wooden bench set against the far wall of the room they had entered was a collection of canteens, old-style Army helmets, and even a few belt buckles. On the floor beneath these

121

carefully arranged items were the rotting remains of gas masks, their corrugated rubber breathing tubes twined together like a den of warmth-seeking snakes. And when the oval glass eyepieces in the crumbling canvas masks reflected the light from Chad's battery lantern, it seemed all the more like a grouping of some inhuman creatures infesting the dark recesses beneath the bench.

Without realizing she was doing so, Alana issued a low moan of fear.

His own skin covered by goose bumps, Roy nonetheless stepped over to the bench, poking under it with a stick he had picked up from the floor. "See, it's nothing but a bunch of old gas masks," he said as soon as he was certain his voice wouldn't betray his nervousness.

"Imagination—remember?" Chad told Alana as he put a reassuring arm around her trembling shoulders. "That's all it is—imagination that makes something perfectly harmless seem so threatening."

Alana nodded but her voice was far from calm when she said, "I know they're just gas masks, Chad. I can see that now. But the place still gives me the creeps."

"Me too," Chad admitted. "But I'm much more curious now than scared. And I've got some questions about this place that I'd like answered before we leave."

"Like who collected all these pieces of Army gear,"

Andy spoke up, "then arranged them so neatly on that bench."

Absorbed in their conversation, they did not notice Roy go into the room adjoining the one where they were standing. But then his excited shout echoed through the house, and they rushed into the other room to find him lifting a rusted bayonet.

"It's . . . it's a whole arsenal of old-time weapons!" he shouted. "Parts of rifles, a couple of pistols, lots of bayonets, some shell casings, and even an old cannon."

For several minutes they busied themselves examining the contents of the room, until Roy tapped Chad on the shoulder. "You notice anything in particular about all these weapons?" the dark-haired boy asked.

"You mean that all of them are badly rusted or otherwise damaged?" Chad asked. When Roy nodded, Chad went on, "Yes, I noticed it too. I'd say they're all pieces that were lost or discarded by the Army when they abandoned Camp Gray Owl."

"So it wasn't the Army who put them all in here?" Sue asked. "I thought maybe they might have stored them here and then forgot to come back for them."

"Not likely," Chad replied.

"Then who . . ." Alana was staring wide-eyed at Chad.

None of the other adventurers had an answer to

Alana's unfinished question, and it was with bemused expressions on their faces that they followed Roy into a narrow hallway, then into a third room at the end of the corridor.

The largest of the three downstairs rooms, this one covered the entire front half of the house and was crowded with several long tables and a conglomeration of packing cases. In one corner the boards had been removed from a grimy-paned window, in front of which stood a rickety desk and chair. Beside these two pieces of furniture an old door had been placed flat atop two sawhorses, and was covered by rows of small objects.

The identity of these objects was revealed to the five young people as soon as they reached the makeshift table, which was bathed in a dust-speckled shaft of light coming in through the unboarded window.

"Arrowheads!" Andy exclaimed.

"Dozens of 'em too!" Sue joined in. "It's a real treasure!"

"There're some pieces of pottery down here," Roy added from the foot of the table. "Looks like there are a few stone tools as well."

Roy then went over to the rickety desk by the window. Spread out on its splintered top like some giant jigsaw puzzle were dozens of clay fragments. Still other dozens of these fragments had been glued together, revealing that someone had been painstakingly reconstructing a broken pottery jar.

Roy was about to share his find with the others when the light coming in through the unboarded window was suddenly obliterated. Looking up, all that Roy could see was a huge figure standing just outside the window. It seemed to be that of a man, but Roy could not be sure. For the late afternoon sun was in back of the hulking form, keeping its face in shadow, while inhuman growls rumbled through the air like thunder.

These menacing growls caused the four others at the table to lift their heads in unison—just in time to see the lower half of the window being raised. Immobilized by shock, they breathlessly watched the huge figure thrust first one leg and then the other over the low sill of the window.

"It's the ghost of Camp Gray Owl!" Sue's terrorized cry rang out over the rumbling growls. "The ghost has come to get us all!"

15

*The Ghost
of Camp Gray Owl*

Sue's shriek momentarily halted the huge figure lum-
bering toward the transfixed teenagers. Even the growling ebbed into a heavy panting. Then suddenly another
sound filled the dusty air of the long-abandoned building—a sound that was as startling as the growls had
been, merely because this new sound was so totally
unexpected.

It was laughter! Rich, rumbling laughter that rolled
over them in rapid waves.

At the same instant, Chad's battery lantern—which
had been dangling forgotten from his fingers—swung
upward to illuminate the source of the new sound.

"Ohhhhh . . ." Sue's drawn-out murmur was echoed
by her four companions as the bright beam of light
revealed the tallest, broadest man any of them had
ever seen before.

Thick, straight, coal-black hair capped the man's

126

massive head, which was thrown back in laughter. Deep wrinkles curved out from the corners of the eyes, which were squinted shut with the mirth that was rumbling up from his thickly muscled throat.

"He . . . he must be crazy!" Andy choked out, grabbing his sister's arm to propel her away from the wildly laughing giant.

Andy's cry brought the others out of their shock-induced immobility.

"The door!" Chad hissed. "Let's try for the door." He spun around, his leg muscles flexed for the race to the doorway of the room. But Chad never took the first step.

Blocking the doorway was a large, silver-gray animal, its bared fangs gleaming yellowish-white in the light from the lantern Chad held in his trembling hand. It was from this animal that the frightening growls started up again, this time punctuated by throaty snarls of unmistakable menace.

"Quiet, Wolf."

The two words were softly spoken, but had the same effect as if they had been shouted. The growls ceased abruptly, and the animal relaxed its tense stance. But the silver-gray form did not move from the doorway, and its watchful eyes remained fixed on the five young people.

Behind them, a deep voice explained. "He's not really

a wolf, even though he may look like one. He's half husky, which accounts for his color. The other half is German shepherd, which I guess gives Wolf his size."

The five adventurers turned to face the tall man, who was wiping away the tears his earlier burst of laughter had left in the corners of his eyes. Having accomplished this, he smiled at them briefly, then turned to light a kerosene lamp on a nearby table.

"As for being crazy, I'm not," he went on in the same conversational tone. "I just couldn't help laughing at the young lady's remark. For I'm not the ghost of Camp Gray Owl either."

"Then . . . then who . . . who are you?" Sue managed, peering around from behind her brother's protective body.

"My name is Charles Longbow," the tall stranger replied. Then he paused as if awaiting their response. When none came, he asked, "And who are you?"

By this time Chad had recovered enough of his composure to introduce himself and his companions. To each name, the black-haired man nodded somberly, then said, "Now that we know each other, perhaps it is time to find out what you are doing here."

The gentle manner of the huge man had emboldened Andy, who blurted out, "What about you? What're you doing here?"

128

Dark, piercing eyes came down to meet the boy's challenging gaze. "I belong here," Charles Longbow said simply.

Alana was the first to grasp the meaning of the tall man's words, for ever since she had heard his name she had been concentrating on Charles Longbow's features—the straight, pitch-black hair and the burnished skin stretched taut over high cheekbones.

"You must be an Indian," she said. "One of the Indians who used to live here."

Charles Longbow nodded. "You are half right. I am an Indian. But I never lived here until about a year ago. I was born and raised in Michigan."

"But your ancestors . . ." Roy began, taking up the thread of Alana's thought.

"Ah, yes, my ancestors—they did once live here, including Chief Gray Owl." And he looked straight at Sue when he said this.

"Then you're the one who's been scaring us!" the younger girl accused.

A smile played at the corners of the tall man's mouth. "Maybe I have," he admitted. "Maybe Wolf has too," and he pointed to the silver-gray dog still sitting in the doorway. "But nothing we did was for the sake of cruelty or to hurt you."

"You just did it to scare us away, huh?" Sue flared. "So you could have all these art-tracks all to yourself!

Well, this is still public land and we've got as much right to be here as you do. We've probably got a better reason too!"

Sue might have said more, had it not been for Andy clamping his hand over her mouth. "Shut up," he pleaded, "before that temper of yours gets us all in trouble."

However, Sue's verbal explosion had no noticeable effect on the man who towered above her. "Again, only half correct," he said softly. "You, indeed, have as much right to be here as I do. But I think my reason is equally as important as yours."

"How can you say that?" the undaunted Sue shot back as soon as Andy had taken his hand away from her lips. "You don't even know why we're here!"

Charles Longbow did not answer, but there was a tolerant kind of smile on his face that made Sue frown, as if she wasn't quite as positive as she had been.

"What *is* your reason for being here?" Roy broke the uncomfortable silence that ensued after Sue spoke. "Are you the one who collected all these?" And the black-haired boy gestured toward the artifact-laden tables.

"Yes, I have collected everything that is here," Charles Longbow replied. "Your other question cannot be answered so simply, however. Perhaps you would like to come upstairs with me. We could talk . . ."

"You mean you don't want to get rid of us?" Sue broke in. "Make us go home?"

One of the man's heavy black eyebrows arched upward. "Get rid of you?" he repeated. "What would be the sense in doing that? You already know much about Camp Gray Owl."

"Including your secret stash!" Andy muttered suspiciously.

"It is not my fault that it is a secret," the Indian answered promptly, but he did not elaborate on what he meant. Instead, he gestured toward the doorway where his dog still kept watch. "Come. We will talk upstairs," he added as he stepped through the doorway, with Wolf in the lead.

Glances were exchanged between the five friends, but not one of them made a move to follow the strange man and his dog.

"Are you coming?" Charles Longbow called from the hallway.

Roy shrugged. "Why not?" he said to the other four. "That guy interests me."

That was all Sue had to hear. "We're coming," she called out to the man already ascending the stairs to the second floor. Then she added in a low tone that only her companions could hear, "I don't think he's dangerous. He only looks that way 'cause he's so awfully big."

131

"Well, I wouldn't like to tangle with him," Andy muttered. "Or that dog."

· "I kind of like both of them," Alana whispered. "And he might tell us more about Camp Gray Owl."

"Better yet, he might even give us some of those art-tracks," Sue said hopefully, as she led the way to the rickety staircase in the hallway.

Charles Longbow was at the topmost step. Above him, a skylight in the roof allowed a dusty shaft of sunlight to penetrate the otherwise gloomy upstairs hall. "Don't be worried about the stairs," he told the five young people still in the lower hall. "They may creak a lot, but they're sturdy."

"They'd have to be if you can go up them safely," Roy said when he had followed his friends to the top of the steps. Then fearing the man might take offense at his remark, Roy added, "I mean . . . I mean you're a pretty muscular guy."

The Indian smiled. "I am also a lot heavier than in the days when I played football and hockey."

"Amateur or professional?" Roy asked, immediately interested.

"I played in college," Longbow replied.

"That's what I had hoped to do," Roy said, his voice taking on a note of bitterness.

"I know."

Roy looked up quickly, a questioning expression in

his dark blue eyes. But Charles Longbow had turned to walk into a nearby room, and Roy could not be sure that he had correctly heard the two softly spoken words. Nor did he have time to question the huge man, for the others were already exclaiming over the contents of the room Longbow had led them into.

16

◁————————*Longbow's Story*

Reds, yellows, browns, blues, and greens—bursts of color were made even brighter by their contrast with the drab, paint-flaked walls on which the Indian items hung. There were not many—a small rug tacked up on the wall next to which a sagging cot held a sleeping bag; a painting of a tribal dance; a long, feather-hung ceremonial pipe with its polished catlinite bowl glowing reddish-brown on the opposite wall; and a small drum with dyed leather thongs securing the decorated deer-hide stretched across both ends. These were the only possessions which told of Charles Longbow's heritage. But they were enough to make the five adventurers want to know more about the strange man who chose to live alone in an abandoned Army camp.

There were no chairs, so Alana and Sue sat on the cot while the others took places on the floor. A silence had fallen over the group, as if now that they had

134

agreed to confer with one another, no one knew where to start. So it was a relief to all of them when Sue pointed to the small drum and asked her host, "Are you a real Indian Indian?" Then amid the chuckles of her friends, Sue added, "What I'm trying to ask is if you play that drum."

Charles Longbow nodded. "Sometimes I do. It can get lonely here, especially at night, with only Wolf to keep me company. So I play the drum and chant the songs I learned as a boy in Michigan. And yes, Sue, I am a real Indian Indian."

"If it's so lonely, then why do you stay here?" Andy wanted to know.

"Because Camp Gray Owl is important to me—just as it is to you."

Andy seemed satisfied with the man's answer, but Sue was not. "You said something like that before. How do you know that it's important to us?"

Charles Longbow sighed faintly. "Because ever since you first came here, Wolf and I have been watching you, sometimes listening to you, and . . ."

"And trying to scare us away from the place!" Andy supplied his own ending for the man's sentence. "Why?"

"Because Camp Gray Owl can be dangerous," the man replied. "For example, two years ago, someone fell into the swamp and was killed."

Sue frowned in remembrance. "That's right. A man did die here. Did . . . did you . . ."

"Did I have anything to do with it?" Charles Longbow smiled briefly. "No, I didn't have anything to do with it, Sue. I wasn't even here at the time. But I wish I had been. Wolf or I might have been able to save him."

Chad's eyes opened widely. "Was it . . . was it you who saved me when I fell off the tunnel wall?"

The five friends waited expectantly for the answer, only to be disappointed when Longbow told them, "We can discuss that later. Right now I think it is more important for us to talk about why you are here and what you intend to do about what you have learned. To start with, why don't you tell me how you found out about Camp Gray Owl and its many legends?"

Sue looked as if she were about to object, but Alana interceded, saying, "I think that would be a good place to start. And since you were responsible for all of this, Sue, why don't you tell Mr. Longbow about it?"

"Just call me Longbow, please," the man said with one of his disarming smiles. "All of you."

"Okay, Longbow," Sue grinned back, and began her story of how she had overheard her father talking to the Parks Commissioner about the state possibly selling the land to a private developer for a housing complex.

Longbow frowned thoughtfully when he heard this,

but he did not speak until Sue finished telling him what she had learned about the history of Camp Gray Owl, as well as its ghost.

"I myself have never encountered any ghosts here," Longbow began, "but I do know that on his deathbed my grandfather, Gray Owl, placed a curse on the camp. And I'm sure that if it were possible for him to come back here as a ghost, he would have done so, for he would have gone to any lengths to prevent the destruction of our ancestral home."

"But you said you were from Michigan, didn't you?" Sue questioned.

"Yes, I am," Longbow replied, "but my people originally came from this area. It was only in the last century that they were forced to give up their land and migrate west. They settled in Michigan, where my father and grandfather and even my great-grandfather were born."

"You mean Gray Owl wasn't born here? Then why . . ." Alana did not finish her sentence, for Longbow had raised his hand palm upward.

"Give me a chance to explain," he told her, then resumed his story. "Toward the end of his life, my grandfather grew more and more concerned about our people. He felt they had been illegally dispossessed from their rightful home and that because of this they were abandoning their Indian heritage. He thought that if they could return to the land of their ancestors, everything would be all right again. This became an obsession with him, and when he could not convince anyone to return here, he came alone."

Longbow sighed sadly. "The rest of the story you know."

"Except where you fit in," Chad pointed out.

"Ah, yes, my presence at Camp Gray Owl—you would wish to know about that. But first let me offer you something to drink on this hot afternoon. I'll be right back."

Longbow had been sitting on the floor with one leg stretched out and the other bent at the knee. In getting up, he almost stumbled, and a silver-gray form rushed to his side. "I'm all right, Wolf," Longbow said as he patted the dog's head. Then he walked toward the door, turning when he reached it. "By the way, Wolf understands that you are friends now. So if you'd like to play with him, I know he'd enjoy a little romp."

This was exactly how they spent the few minutes that Longbow was out of the room. Just as he had said, the dog was now a friendly playmate, instead of the growling menace they had first encountered downstairs, and all were laughing heartily over Wolf's antics when Longbow returned.

Passing out paper cups, Longbow began to pour something from a moisture-beaded jug. "I've had this birch beer cooling in the well behind the house," he began, only to stop when Sue held her palm over the top of her cup.

"None for me, thank you," she said primly. "I'm not allowed to drink beer."

There was a second or two of silence. Then the Indian threw back his huge head and his rumbling laugh erupted, quickly joined by the hilarity of the four oldest adventurers.

"I don't see anything so funny about refusing to drink beer," the younger girl snapped, only to be greeted by fresh gusts of glee.

Longbow, however, had managed to quell his laughter. "Dear Sue," he said gently, "birch beer is not real beer. It has no alcoholic content. It's just a soft drink that tastes a lot like sarsaparilla."

"Then they shouldn't call it beer!" Sue sniffed, but there was a grin on her face when she handed over her cup to be filled.

Once they had drunk their fill of the pleasantly cool birch beer, which Longbow told them he had made himself, the five adventurers sat back down to listen to the rest of the Indian's story.

"I had not even been born yet when my grandfather left Michigan," Longbow resumed. "But the story of what happened to him was always told whenever there was a tribal gathering."

"Did you live in a teepee in Michigan?" Sue couldn't

help interrupting. "And did you wear a feathered head-dress and moccasins and shoot a bow and arrow?"

Longbow shook his head, smiling patiently. "None of those things, Sue," he replied. "We lived in a regular house and wore clothing just like yours—except, of course, when we attended Indian ceremonies and such."

"Ohhhhh." Sue's disappointment was obvious.

"In fact," Longbow went on, "I was just like all of you, going to a regular high school, engaging in sports, and then going on to college. I had my whole future planned out, and if it hadn't been for the war in Vietnam, I might have accomplished all the things I wanted to do. But there was a war, I was drafted, and everything changed."

"What happened?" Roy asked.

"This," the Indian said simply, reaching along his outstretched left leg to pull up the cuff of his jeans. Below the edge of the faded denim the flesh-colored plastic of an artificial limb gleamed softly in the waning afternoon sunlight coming in through the windows.

"Gee, who . . . who would have ever known?" Sue's stammered words broke the silence that followed Long-bow's revelation. "You . . . you don't limp or any-thing."

The tall man pulled his cuff back down, then slowly

got to his feet. "Yes," he said, "I learned the physical part quickly. It was the emotional adjustment that took time."

"I can imagine how hard it must have been," Alana sympathized.

"Forgive me, but I don't think that you can," Longbow corrected her gently. "Only someone who suffers such a handicap truly understands how difficult it is to accept it, especially if that handicap smashes all his dreams."

"Is that what happened to you?" Andy asked.

Longbow nodded. "I wasted years feeling sorry for myself, wandering from one place to another, never attempting any of the many things I was still capable of accomplishing. Then one of my wandering trips took me to the Northeast, and I came here to see the home of my ancestors."

Pausing to smile at Sue, Longbow continued, "Perhaps it was the spirit of Gray Owl—maybe even his ghost—but here I found a new dream, a new direction, a new purpose for living. But now this dream is threatened with destruction too."

A sudden whine from Wolf made everybody jump. But the dog was only reacting to his master's unhappy tone, and he began dancing around Longbow's feet as if to cheer him.

141

"You're absolutely right, Wolf," Longbow said as he bent down to pet the silver-gray head. "It's time to stop such glum talk." Then looking toward the window, he added, "It's also time for you young people to start for home. I wouldn't want you to risk walking through Camp Gray Owl after dusk. It really is dangerous, you know."

"And how we know!" Sue declared, and immediately picked up her backpack.

"But we haven't talked nearly enough," came Alana's complaint.

"I'll walk with you to the edge of the swamp," Longbow offered, "and we can talk more along the way. Then, too, you can always come back here again— that is, as long as this is still public land, which I fear may not be the case for very much longer."

For the first time since Longbow had shown them his artificial leg, Roy spoke. "They just couldn't sell this place for a housing development! It would destroy everything!"

"Well, as I said, that sometimes happens to the dreams we have."

Roy's heavy black eyebrows were drawn together as he followed Longbow from the room. "You spoke of an earlier dream," he reminded the older man. "What kind of dream was it that you had before you got hurt in Vietnam?"

Longbow glanced back over his shoulder at the dark-haired boy. "My earlier dream?" he repeated. "I had wanted to be a professional hockey player." Then without another word, he continued down the stairs, leaving Roy to stare at his retreating back.

17

◁———————*A Shadowy Trail*
. . . An Enlightening Talk

The sun had already disappeared behind the trees to the west, and even though the sky overhead was still a bright blue, the dense forest through which they walked was dark and threatening.

"I see what you mean about getting out of Camp Gray Owl before nightfall," Chad said to Longbow. "Even with a flashlight, I wouldn't want to try to find my way through here after dark."

Longbow nodded. "I think that might have been what happened to the real-estate man who died in the swamp. He may have remained here too late looking over the land, then stumbled into the swamp in the dark."

"But the newspaper report said there was only a couple of inches of water in the swamp," Sue pointed out, as she brushed past Chad to walk beside Longbow.

"How could anyone drown in that little amount of water?"

"Maybe he hit his head on a rock," Andy offered. "What do you think, Longbow?"

"That's possible," the tall man said, looking back at Andy, who was in the rear of their small procession. "It's also possible he happened into a patch of quicksand, for there are such places in the swamp." Next to him, Sue shivered, and Longbow assured her, "None of those patches of quicksand is deep, and you can get out of them if you keep your head. But if someone panics, as that man may have done . . ."

Longbow's words trailed off and it was several moments before he went on. "As I said, Camp Gray Owl can be dangerous to someone unfamiliar with it. But then, even the sounds of the forest at night can be frightening to anyone not used to them."

"They can be frightening in the daytime too," Alana spoke up. "Especially owls that hoot when they're not supposed to."

"You mean like this?" Longbow asked. And cupping his hands to his mouth, he emitted several throaty calls like the ones they had heard from time to time on their way through Camp Gray Owl.

A sudden thrashing noise in the underbrush nearby startled the five adventurers, but Longbow remained unperturbed. A few seconds later, Wolf came bounding across a fallen log to stand panting in front of his master.

"Hey, that's neat!" laughed Andy. "Instead of whistling at Wolf to get him to come to you, you hoot like an owl."

"And that way anyone who is within hearing distance doesn't know that you're around—right, Longbow?"

The tall man nodded to what Chad said.

"Did you also do it because of the legend about what happens if the owl hoots in the daytime?" Sue asked.

Again Longbow nodded, this time somewhat sheepishly. "It is an old superstition that an owl hooting in the daytime means trouble. But I also read about it when I did some research on Camp Gray Owl at the state library. I thought that my hooting might discourage some people from coming here, for I preferred to keep my presence a secret. That way no one would interfere with my work until I was ready."

"Ready for what?" Roy asked.

"Ready to present full evidence of the historical importance of Camp Gray Owl—that is, if I ever found a public official who would listen to me."

By now the group had emerged from the woods and they were standing at the western side of the third tunnel, where the steps led down to the underpass.

Gesturing for the others to sit with him on the steps, Longbow suggested, "Let us take a few minutes' rest. It is getting late, I know, but you still have time before it is fully dark. I only wish my jeep was in working order. Then I could drive all of you home. But the jeep is being repaired at a garage in Olmsville."

"Olmsville?" Sue echoed.

"A village about six miles south of here," Longbow told her. "It's not a big community, but it's got a grocery store and a garage—enough for my needs."

"So that's why we've never seen you in High Falls, where we live," Chad mused. "I was wondering about that, as well as how you got your food, but I never thought of Olmsville. What do you do, park the jeep on the highway near the trail we came in on, and then carry your supplies to the camp from there?"

Longbow shook his head. "There is an old road that leads into the camp from the west. It's all overgrown, but my jeep can get through. It was a road the Army built to bring equipment and men into the camp."

"I should have known there had to be a road!" Roy exclaimed, slapping his right leg in emphasis. Then he grimaced when a twinge of pain reminded him that he had jostled his injured knee. But Roy was too intent on what was being said to pay more than a second's attention to the flash of pain that passed as quickly as it came.

"I'll show you the road the next time you come," Longbow offered.

"You mean you really would like us to come back?"

Longbow looked at the youngest member of the group. "Yes, Sue, I really mean it." Then his dark eyes focused on Roy. "Perhaps some of you would like to help me in cataloguing all that I have collected before it is too late."

There was an excited chorus of affirmative replies—except for Roy, who remained silently staring in front of him, a deep frown on his face. And when he finally spoke, his words had nothing to do with returning to Camp Gray Owl. Instead, he asked, "Do you honestly believe the state would sell this land for a housing development? I mean, once you tell them how important it is . . ."

"I tried telling them a year ago," Longbow explained. "But the man in charge would not listen. All he said was that it was totally useless to the state, and dangerous as well. That if someone else died or got hurt here the state might be liable for a great deal of money. It would be better, he told me, if the state sold the land—got rid of it."

"But didn't you tell him about its historic value—not just because it was an Army camp, but about your people?" Alana wanted to know.

148

"Of course, but my words meant nothing. I was just some stranger from Michigan. I had no expertise—I think that was the word he used. I had no degree in archaeology or history. Nor did I have any proof about my people—just old legends."

"So you began gathering proof," Chad murmured, his voice full of admiration.

"And in the meantime you tried to keep people away from here so they wouldn't get hurt," Sue added.

Longbow nodded as he rose to his feet. "Yes, Wolf always alerts me when there are strangers in the area. We keep watch from the woods whenever someone is near the swamp . . ."

"Then it was you we heard yesterday when we were sitting on the wall by the swamp!" Without waiting for an answer, Sue rushed on, "And it was you who almost scared me to death in the tunnel. You know, that wasn't very nice, Longbow. I could have been killed if I fell off that rusty old staircase frame in the tower!"

A little angry at whom she considered responsible for her terrifying experience of the day before, Sue ignored the outstretched hand Longbow was offering to help her up from her seat on the concrete steps.

"I had nothing to do with what happened to you in the tunnel," Longbow said earnestly. "When all of you went into the tunnel the first time, I waited around to make sure you came back out safely. When you did, I went back to my work in the old command post, thinking you'd be returning home—that's what I heard you say you were going to do. But just to make sure, I left Wolf to watch you."

Sue's eyes lit up in understanding. "It must have been Wolf who followed me in the tunnel!" And she turned to face her brother. "See, Andy, I wasn't just imagining things! Wolf must have come in through that hole in the floor next to the tunnel wall. Even though he's a pretty big dog, he could have squeezed through that!"

"So you aren't totally crazy," Andy said dryly. "Just slightly nuts!"

Chad put one hand on Sue's shoulder and the other on Andy's, then gave both of them a shake. "Okay, okay, let's not start the bickering business, you two. I'd rather hear what else Longbow has to say."

"I had no idea you had gone back into the tunnel, Sue," Longbow resumed, "or that you four had to rescue her from the framework in the tower. Wolf came to get me, but by the time I reached the entrance to the tunnel, you were already back out again. Only then did I learn what happened to you inside, when I overheard you talking about it."

Sue's gray eyes were downcast as she got up from

the step. "Longbow, I'm sorry for what I said about you," she murmured.

The tall man gave no reply, but once more extended his hand to the girl. This time Sue took it, and together they started off along the western side of the tunnel wall, with the four others following along behind.

As they walked north through the woods, paralleling the third tunnel, Longbow explained how he had been the one who had shoveled in the dirt and stones to form the barricade they had discovered between the second and third tunnel. "I thought that mound of earth would keep people from exploring further," he went on. "I never imagined anyone would think of entering the third tunnel by going through the hole in the roof by the target wall. It seems I underestimated you though." And he turned to smile at Chad and Andy.

"That third tunnel is terribly unsafe, however, and I hope you don't enter it again," Longbow added as an afterthought.

"Oh, you don't have to worry about that," Andy assured him. "One trip inside that tunnel convinced me—and I'm sure Chad was more than convinced when he fell off the top of it!"

Chad had been walking next to Alana, behind the other four, but when Andy said this he hurried forward to confront Longbow. "It was you who gave me a

151

boost up when I was hanging from the tree, wasn't it?"

"Yes."

"That's what I figured," Chad said. "What I can't figure out, though, is how you did it. I mean, how you did it without me seeing you."

Before Longbow could answer, Alana's slightly scolding voice reached Chad's ears. "And what I can't figure out is why, if you knew Longbow saved you, you haven't thanked him before this."

Somewhat embarrassed, Chad murmured, "I guess I owe you an apology too, Longbow. I should have thanked you earlier for saving my life."

"Well, I don't know if it was a matter of life or death," the Indian answered modestly. "But at least you didn't get hurt." Then he went on to explain how he had followed their progress by staying on the eastern side of the tunnel wall while Andy and Chad were exploring the interior.

"So it was your shadow we saw through the crack in the wall just before we got to the spot where the tree grows out of the hole in the roof!"

Longbow nodded. "I was walking quite close to the wall at that point, for the crack you spoke of occurs where the land is still level with the base of the tunnel. Just a few feet south of there, it dips sharply down into that rock-filled ravine where Chad almost fell."

152

Andy breathed a long sigh. "You know, when I saw that shadow, I was almost convinced that Camp Gray Owl is haunted, just like . . ."

"But it is!"

The three short words brought the group to an abrupt halt.

"Now I know for sure this place is haunted!" Sue went on in a tremulous tone. "Just look at those lights over there!"

18

◁───────────────── *The Spirits*
Dance at Twilight

Within the shadowy depths of a jagged crack in the nearby tunnel wall, a glowing mass could be seen. Surrounding this shimmering shapeless mass, smaller specks of light appeared then disappeared, as if suddenly snuffed out by some supernatural force.

"It's the ghost of Camp Gray Owl!" Sue moaned in a way that was almost as eerie as the glow coming from within the tunnel wall.

Sue had already spun around, to race away from the frightening object, when Longbow's strong fingers closed around her wrist.

"It is not the ghost of Gray Owl," he said sharply. "It is not a ghost at all."

"But . . . but . . ." the girl sputtered, trying to pull away from his grasp. But Longbow would not let go.

"There is nothing supernatural about the light you

154

see," the tall man went on in a softer tone. "Come with me and I will show you."

For a moment, Sue resisted the pull on her wrist, but when Andy and the others came up alongside her, then passed her on their way over to the tunnel wall, Sue allowed Longbow to lead her there.

They were still several feet away from the crack in the tunnel wall when some of the small specks of light sailed toward Sue, flashing on and off as they did so.

"Fireflies!" she exclaimed. "That's all they are—fireflies!"

"Also called lightning bugs," Longbow told her. "You see, Sue, there is usually a perfectly natural explanation for most things that may at first seem completely unnatural."

"Even . . . even for that?" Sue asked, pointing toward the crack in the tunnel wall where the glowing mass was still evident.

"Even that," Longbow assured her. Stepping over to where the other four were peering into the opening, Longbow gestured for Roy to direct his flashlight beam inside.

The bright shaft of light revealed nothing more mysterious than the rotting stump of a tree.

"Now turn off your flashlight."

Roy did as Longbow requested, and within seconds

the strange glow appeared again where the tree stump was located.

"It's called bioluminescence," Longbow explained, "and it's caused by certain insects inside that rotting stump. I'm sure you've all heard of a glowworm, haven't you? Well, that's the general term for any insect larva that is bioluminescent."

Sue was still staring at the glowing tree stump. "Bio . . . bio . . ." she began. "Nope, that's one word I don't think my tongue can handle."

"Too bad," Andy quipped. "I was waiting to hear how you'd mangle a word like biolulu . . . bioluna . . . biolulo . . ."

"My dear brother, are you trying to say bioluminescence?" Sue carefully pronounced the difficult word, then grinned in triumph at Andy.

When the others had stopped laughing, Longbow said, "Unlike the kind of light that produces heat, such as fire or even a light bulb, bioluminescence generates almost no heat. Therefore, scientists call it 'cold light'— which is easier for everybody to pronounce, including me."

"Cold light," Sue repeated. "And I thought it was a ghost!"

Longbow smiled. "It is only human to think of something as being supernatural when you have no other explanation for it. My own people used to think that

156

fireflies were the spirits of dead people who returned to dance on a summer's night. They also told of seeing ghost bears that glowed in the dark. A more scientific explanation might be that those ghost bears were just ordinary animals that had been poking around in a tree stump looking for grubs and worms to eat. The bears could have picked up some bioluminescent larvae on their paws and snouts, and that is what made them glow."

As Longbow was speaking, Roy had caught a lightning bug in his cupped-together hands. After looking at it a moment, he released it to fly away in the deepening twilight. Then he turned to the tall man. "How come you know so much about things like cold light?"

"I was a zoology major in college," Longbow replied, as he began walking north with Sue and Andy beside him.

Alana and Chad hurried to catch up with the other four, who by now had reached the place where the second and third tunnels met the target wall.

"Then I guess you could tell us a lot more about the *natural* aspects of Camp Gray Owl," Alana speculated, having overheard Longbow's last remark.

The tall man smiled at her emphasis of the word "natural." Then a wistful expression replaced the smile as he said, "Having lain abandoned for so long, this place is like a vast natural laboratory where people could come to learn about wildlife and . . ."

Cutting off his words, Longbow pulled himself up to the top of the wall, then reached down to help Sue. "I think we will make better time if we walk along the top of the second tunnel," he told the others. "Just be careful to stay away from the edge."

"That reminds me," Chad said as he gained the top of the tunnel. "You never did tell us how you managed to stay out of sight when you rescued me."

The sky overhead had darkened considerably since they had set out from the command post. However, because of its height, the top of the tunnel was above much of the dense vegetation, and there was enough light for them to see where they were going without using their flashlights.

As they walked in single file, Longbow raised his usually low-keyed voice enough for all of them to hear his explanation of how he had rescued Chad.

At the time Chad fell off the top of the third tunnel, Longbow had already descended into the narrow, rock-filled ravine that bordered the eastern side of the wall. But when the boy first looked down, Longbow had not yet reached the area directly beneath the tree Chad was hanging on to. Chad had not looked down again until after Longbow's powerful arm had provided the force for Chad to regain the top of the tunnel. And by the time he did, Longbow had slipped into the crack in the tunnel wall on the southern side of the tree. From there, Longbow had made his way south through the crumbling tunnel to the underpass, then on to the command post.

For a second time, Longbow had assumed the group would return home—and for a second time he had been wrong. For shortly after he reached the command post, Longbow was warned by Wolf's low-pitched growls that the strangers were approaching. Man and dog had set off through the woods, circling around to where Longbow thought the young people might be.

Never suspecting the five adventurers had spotted the command post's twin chimneys over the tops of the trees, Longbow had planned only to watch the intruders, and perhaps try to distract them by making thrashing noises in the woods if they got too close to the command post. The young people had moved faster than he anticipated, however. Having found the vague trail to the command post, they reached it well before Longbow and Wolf completed their circuit through the dense underbrush.

"I probably couldn't have scared you anyway," Longbow concluded. "You just don't scare easily."

"Oh, I don't know about that," Alana laughed. "We've been plenty scared a couple of times since we came to Camp Gray Owl."

By this time they had reached the northern end of the second tunnel and had turned east along the narrow target wall which led to the tower. Pointing to it, Longbow said, "I believe those two rooms next to the tower were probably like offices—at least I found a lot of equipment when I went digging around in there."

"No wonder we never found anything around here," Sue commented mournfully. "Longbow's swept the place clean."

"Hardly," he demurred. "There is still much to be discovered in Camp Gray Owl—many questions to be answered. But not today. Today, we'd better concentrate on getting you home. I see the evening star has already appeared." And Longbow pointed up to where a single twinkling light could be seen in the now indigo-colored sky. "That means night is not far away."

Lowering his massive body to the ground below, Longbow turned to catch Sue as she scooted off the top of the target wall. The others quickly followed, and they made their way through the room next to the tower, and the tower itself. Sue apprehensively glanced up at the rusted staircase as the beam from Roy's flashlight swept the tower room, but she did not say anything about her earlier ordeal. She only looked at Roy, who gave her shoulder an understanding

160

pat. Then they left the tower to proceed north through the first tunnel.

As they passed by the shallow box attached to the inside of the tunnel wall, Chad asked Longbow about it. The tall man said he thought it had been used to house a field telephone or some other communication device. He was only guessing, however, he told them, since the box was already empty when he first came across it.

Little else was said during their trip through the tunnel, except for Sue pointing out the hole in the floor where she thought Wolf had entered. As if to confirm her guess, the big dog obligingly wriggled down into the hole, gave a few short barks when he had emerged on the other side of the tunnel wall, then came slithering back through the hole to follow them to the tunnel's end.

Climbing up the steps that led to the concrete walk-way alongside the first of the target walls, Alana looked up at Longbow, who had paused on the top step. "Do you ever get the feeling that Camp Gray Owl really is haunted?" she asked. "Even though there is a logical explanation for most of the things that have happened here?"

"My people have always believed there are such things as ghosts," Longbow answered vaguely.

161

"And curses," Alana persisted. "Do you think this place really could be cursed?"

Again Longbow was vague. "My grandfather believed he could do so."

The frown on Alana's face revealed she was far from satisfied with Longbow's answer, but she did not press him further. Instead, she said, "Well, if there is such a thing as a curse on Camp Gray Owl, maybe we can do something about getting it lifted."

"Don't you think the Army already did that by moving out?" Andy said. "That was what the curse was all about, wasn't it?"

Alana shook her head. "Not quite. As I see it, there's still more to be done before old Gray Owl will be satisfied—a lot more."

19

The Curse Is Lifted

When the five adventurers had said good-bye to Long-bow the night before, Alana had promised they would return the following day. She had not revealed to him a plan that had been forming in her mind during the walk back through Camp Gray Owl that evening, but she did confide it to the others as they hiked down the highway toward their homes in High Falls.

All four had been enthusiastic about Alana's plan to bring her father to Camp Gray Owl the next day. As an archaeologist, Professor O'Malley would be interested in the site, and perhaps even be able to help Longbow in saving as many Indian artifacts as possible before the land was sold. Sue's father would also be home since it was the Labor Day weekend, and she and Andy would ask Mr. Gregorio to accompany them. While he had no power to stop the state from selling the land to a private developer, as a member of the

Town Planning Board, Mr. Gregorio might have some ideas on how such a sale could at least be delayed.

Tired from the long day they had spent in the open air, but excited about the prospects of helping their new friend achieve his goal, the five agreed to meet at Alana's home the next morning at ten o'clock.

Chad got there early, as did Andy and Sue, who were accompanied by their father. While Mr. Gregorio and Professor O'Malley discussed what their children had told them, the four young people sat on the front porch awaiting the arrival of Roy.

Ten o'clock came but Roy did not.

At 10:30, Alana called Roy's house. When there was no answer, she confidently told her companions, "Roy must be on his way over here. I know his parents went away for the weekend, so that's why nobody picked up the phone."

But by eleven o'clock, Alana was worried. "It would only take Roy ten minutes to get here from his house, even if he was walking on his hands and knees!"

"Let's give him until 11:30," Professor O'Malley suggested. "If Roy isn't here by then, we'd better leave. We can stop by his house on our way to Camp Gray Owl."

"And also at the football field," Sue spoke up. "Roy sometimes goes there."

The sudden reminder of Roy's depression over his

164

injured knee was like a dark cloud covering their sunny spirits. Well aware of Roy's difficulties, which had been a constant topic of conversation with his daughter Sue, Mr. Gregorio was far from optimistic. "Maybe Roy lost interest," the older man said. "Maybe he's just giving up, as he has with everything else lately."

"I can't believe that," Sue maintained. "I *won't* believe it!"

But she had to consider the possibility when they found no one home at Roy's house, and he was not at the football field either.

"Maybe he hurt himself or something," Sue said, still unwilling to accept what seemed to be a fact— that Roy had no intention of returning with them to Camp Gray Owl.

"And that was our only chance of convincing him not to quit school!" Sue voiced her disappointment as Professor O'Malley backed his car out of the parking lot near the football field and headed south along the highway.

On their way, they stopped to talk to a group of bicyclers, two of whom were neighbors of Roy's. They said they had seen Roy leave his home early that morning, but he had not told them where he was going.

"Did you try his girlfriend's house?" one of the bicyclers called over his shoulder as he pedaled away from Professor O'Malley's car.

None of them had thought about Roy's girlfriend, but it really didn't matter anyway because when they telephoned her from a pay booth at the nearest gas station, the girl said she hadn't seen Roy or spoken to him in several weeks.

Sue actually seemed relieved when she heard this, but the troubled expression returned to her eyes as her companions discussed Roy's problem during the drive to Camp Gray Owl. As soon as they arrived there, however, the topic apparently was forgotten in the meeting of Charles Longbow with two men who immediately grasped the importance of what he was trying to do.

"Although I teach at the state university only twenty miles from here," Professor O'Malley told Longbow, "I had never heard of this being the site of an Indian village."

"Then you think it is important?"

"Absolutely!" came Professor O'Malley's enthusiastic reply. "We know very little about the Indians who inhabited this area. To be able to study such a site would be invaluable."

The three men had been walking along the stream where Sue had picked up the arrowhead, with the other four following close behind, when Longbow pointed to the mound. "There is a tradition among my people that in the early times—before they moved to Michi-

166

gan—they buried their dead in mounds like that."

Professor O'Malley's eyes, which were as blue as those of his daughter Alana, grew wide with anticipation.

"But that may only be a story," Longbow continued. "It appears to me to be more likely that the Army left behind that heap of stones and earth, though I do not know for sure. I never had the time to investigate the mound."

"I'm glad you didn't!" Alana's father told him frankly.

"Because there're snakes!" Sue cried out.

Professor O'Malley smiled at Sue's reasoning. "That's one consideration," he conceded. Then he went on earnestly to Longbow, "More importantly, you could have destroyed an invaluable archaeological site if you had started to dig there."

Seeing Longbow's hurt expression, Professor O'Malley hurried on, "Forgive me for being so blunt. I know you were trying to save all that you could because you feared the land was going to be sold. But a site as important as this might be," and he pointed to the mound, "must be investigated under rigid scientific standards."

"Then it is fortunate I did not touch it," Longbow agreed. "But what will happen if . . ."

Alana's father broke in, "I guarantee you from now

on there won't be any ifs about saving this land. Will there, Dan?" And he turned questioning eyes toward Mr. Gregorio.

Andy and Sue's father shook his head vigorously. "No, sir," he stated. "There have been a lot of changes made at the state level since you first sought help about saving this land, Longbow. The man you spoke to has been replaced by a three-member commission. We've also got a new Department of Environmental Conservation which has the power to protect such sites. Plus that, since Camp Gray Owl lies within the boundaries of our township, even I've got some say in what happens to it. And I sure know what I'm going to say about it!"

The three adults and three teenagers began chattering so excitedly they did not realize Sue had not joined in. It was only when they were walking away from the mound that they realized Sue had not said a word.

"It's Roy that's bothering her," Alana told the three men. "Sue was hoping so hard that Roy would become interested enough in Camp Gray Owl that he'd decide to go back to school." Then she went on to explain to Longbow about Roy's injury preventing him from earning an athletic scholarship to college, and that Roy felt he had no chance of getting high enough grades to qualify for a merit scholarship, especially in Miss Stitt's American history class.

168

Longbow's face was grave. "When you were here that first day, I overheard enough to figure out Roy's problem. Then when we met, I tried to show him, without actually telling him, how important an education is and that a physical handicap does not have to mean the end of all your dreams."

The tall man sighed deeply. "But I was so concerned about my own problem here in Camp Gray Owl that I may not have been very convincing."

"I think you were," Chad stated firmly, "even though I wasn't aware of what you were doing at the time. Why, you even asked Roy to help you with cataloguing your collection. If that didn't convince him, nothing would!"

"And I guess nothing did," Sue gloomily summed up the situation.

Resuming their discussion of Camp Gray Owl, the three men talked about what could be done in the future—how it could be turned into a combination wildlife refuge and historical park, with ongoing archaeological investigations, plus a museum housing both Army memorabilia and Indian artifacts. As for the curator of such a museum, Professor O'Malley and Mr. Gregorio both agreed there could be no other choice than the man whose ancestors had first lived in the area.

Longbow smiled at their compliment, but his victory

169

over saving Camp Gray Owl was shadowed by the apparent loss of Roy. And Longbow's eyes were sad as he led his six companions along a path he had made through the woods. This path would take them on a more direct course to the command post than if they went by way of the target walls and tunnels.

In their concern over Camp Gray Owl and Roy, neither Longbow nor the four adventurers had been aware Wolf was not with them. So it was a surprise to all of them when the silver-gray dog came racing toward them as they emerged from the woods surrounding the command post.

Barking loudly and dancing on his hind feet, Wolf excitedly greeted his master, then raced back and forth between Longbow and the house.

"Someone's in there," the tall man told the others. Then he hurried forward with a worried look on his face.

Before he could reach the command post, a thick-set figure appeared around the corner of the house.

"Roy!" Sue shouted, and ran toward him, only to stop halfway when she saw another figure appear from in back of the house.

"What took you guys so long?" Roy asked, when the group reached him. "Miss Stitt was just about ready to give up and go home." And he gestured toward the elderly woman who had come up alongside him.

"Miss Stitt!" Sue breathed. "The history teacher!"

"She's also the head of the new Department of Environmental Conservation," Roy said. "Last night when I remembered reading about her appointment to that post, I tried to get in touch with her. But her family told me she was spending the weekend up at Tomahawk Lake. So that's where I went early this morning."

Since all the others seemed too shocked to speak, Miss Stitt took a few steps forward. "I must say Roy Benedict is a most persuasive young man," she began. "I wouldn't have thought anyone could convince me to cut short my last vacation before school starts. But then, I always did have a soft spot for anyone planning to major in history or anthropology in college." And she turned to smile at Roy.

"Does that mean . . ." Alana began, only to be interrupted by the exuberant Roy.

"That was the other thing I had to see Miss Stitt about—to tell her I'm not going to quit school."

"Oh, Roy!" was all that Sue could manage to say.

The others, however, were more expressive. Having overcome their initial shock, they gathered around Roy and Miss Stitt, voicing their congratulations at Roy's decision to return to school, and at the same time trying to tell the history teacher about Camp Gray Owl.

"You don't have to convince me as to the importance of this site," the gray-haired woman said sternly, as if she were addressing a class of somewhat boisterous high-school freshmen. "Roy has done quite a thorough job of detailing the merits of Camp Gray Owl."

Then allowing her lips to relax into a smile, the woman added, "And I'll make sure my fellow members in the Department of Environmental Conservation are just as convinced as I am!"

By the time the visitors started for home, great slabs of black shadow had fallen eastward from the crumbling walls of Camp Gray Owl. Yet even with the added darkness, the ominous air that had pervaded the place seemed to have disappeared—a feeling that Alana put into words as they said good-bye to Longbow and Wolf.

"Yes," the tall man replied, "it is as if the curse has been lifted—that is, if there ever was a curse at all."

"There must have been," Sue insisted. "Remember the artillery shells that always wound up in the wrong places? The Army never did figure out why that happened."

When Longbow smiled, she added, "So there may not be a natural explanation for everything."

"Maybe not," Longbow conceded. "But if Camp Gray Owl was haunted, I do not think the ghost is here anymore."

Chad nodded. "And even though my helpful ghost

172

turned out to be a very human being named Longbow, I still say the same thing I did yesterday, only with a slight alteration: that if there ever was a ghost at Camp Gray Owl, it was a good ghost—good for Longbow and good for Roy."

"That reminds me," the black-haired boy spoke up. "Longbow, would it be all right if I brought my girlfriend out to see you next weekend? I'd really like to show her the place where I'll be working on cataloguing those artifacts you've collected so far."

"Of course," the tall man answered immediately, but Longbow's eyes were on Sue as he said it. Nor did his concerned gaze leave the figure of the young girl until she disappeared from sight as the group walked through the woods on their way to the highway, with Roy and Miss Stitt in the lead.

Knowing how Sue felt about Roy, Alana and Chad had been equally worried about the young girl's reaction to Roy's mention of the girl he obviously intended to start seeing again. They hurried to catch up with Sue, only to find Andy walking beside his sister, his arm around her shoulders, but unable to express the words he wanted to say. It was Alana who said them for him.

"Sue," she began, "we're sorry about . . . I mean, we all know how you feel about Roy, and that you were hoping . . ."

Her gray eyes were glassy with unshed tears, but Sue's voice was steady when she raised her head and said, "Well, we won half the battle. We got Roy to go back to school, and that was the most important thing of all."

Then with a saucy bounce of her brown ponytail, Sue added, "As for the other half of the battle, it's not lost yet. Roy's not going to be married for a long time—he'll be going to college now, you see. And in that time I'll be doing some more growing up. So I still have a chance!"

The three other adventurers could only shake their heads in amused wonder as the undaunted Sue skipped ahead up the trail to join Roy and Miss Stitt.